Baker's Bargain
Book Five in Culpepper Cowboys

by Kirsten Osbourne

Baker's Bargain
Book Five in Culpepper Cowboys
by Kirsten Osbourne

Copyright © 2016 Kirsten Osbourne
This book is a work of fiction. Names, characters, places, and incidents are products of the author's imagination or are used fictitiously. Any resemblance to actual events or locales or persons, living or dead, is entirely coincidental.

Cover design by Erin Dameron-Hill

Chapter One

Marcus Wells watched as his client walked out of his office, running his fingers through his hair. Another divorce. He was starting to wonder if people ever really had good marriages, but then he looked at his grandparents, and he knew they did. He wanted that for himself, but there were no single women left in town.

Culpepper, Wyoming, had been victimized by the men's underwear industry. One of the local ranchers had opened up his home for an underwear shoot, and all of the women in town had kindly volunteered their time. When a sudden spring snowstorm blew into town, the women had been stranded with the men. Many weddings had occurred once the roads were passable.

He leaned back in his chair and frowned. The only single ladies who had come to town in years had been the Quinlan Quadruplets, and they'd been spoken for by the four Culpeppers since the day they arrived.

Marcus frowned. He was not a fan of the Culpeppers. The youngest boy, Chris, had been in his class at school. The girls had always fawned over Chris and ignored Marcus, who even then had been very studious. Of course, Chris had been smart too, but in an outdoorsy cowboyish way.

He stood and walked to the small window of his office which looked onto Main Street of Culpepper. He saw Joy Culpepper, formerly Quinlan, leave the grocery store and head to her car. The woman was beautiful and had said something to him about bringing her younger sister out to meet him from Kentucky. He thought for a moment, trying to remember the sister's name. Oh right. Grace.

If she was half as beautiful as her older sisters, then he was more than willing to give it a shot.

He'd never really believed in arranged marriages, but more and more, they seemed like a really good idea to him. He wished he could just call someone and they would send him a bride, complete with dress and veil, ready to walk down the aisle.

He frowned for a moment. Joy had said she would try. He wondered if she'd contacted her sister.

Rushing out the door to his office, he ran across the street. "Do you need help putting your groceries in the truck, Joy?"

Joy looked around and smiled. "Oh, hi, Marcus. I would adore some help. Morning sickness has set in, and I'm just not feeling like doing a whole lot, but for some reason, Kolby still insists on eating."

"What is it with those Culpeppers? They get all the prettiest girls, and then they expect them to cook and clean. They should hire maids for you and put you on pedestals."

Joy laughed. "I wasn't raised to be put on a pedestal."

"Speaking of your raising…did you ever talk to your sister about me?"

"Grace? I did, but it's been a while. They're getting ready to come out here. I can have her meet you for lunch one day."

Marcus nodded. "I'd like that a lot. In fact, get her to agree to marry me as soon as she arrives."

Joy shrugged. "She thought about contacting the matchmaker who set us up with the Culpepper men. I don't think she'd be terribly opposed to meeting you and having a short engagement."

"Really?" He couldn't help but wonder what the girl looked like if she'd be willing to date a stranger. Not that looks mattered too much to him, but he did want to make sure he was attracted to her. "Do you have a picture of her?"

She pulled out her phone and flipped through the photos while he put her groceries onto the backseat of the truck for her. "Oh, here she is!" She held up her phone for him to see her sister Grace.

He looked down at the petite looking blonde on the phone and nodded. "She's pretty." Beautiful was more like it. Absolutely stunning.

"She is. And she's very sweet, and more importantly, she can make the best cakes and cupcakes you've ever tasted. I've been trying to get her to move here and open a bakery."

He nodded slowly. "That would be a great

idea. Right now we only have the small bakery in the grocery store, and they certainly can't provide wedding cakes or anything like that."

"I'm going to call her again tonight and see if I can light a fire under her. I know she's been talking to two of our cousins and her twin about coming with her."

"I can understand bringing her twin, but why the cousins?" Soon the entire population of Culpepper would be outnumbered by the Quinlans.

"Well, our cousins, Patience and Felicity, make pies and cookies. The three of them are perfect business partners. Honor is a bit of a tomboy, much to Mom's horror."

He grinned at that. "Why her horror?" Looking at the pretty girl in front of him, he couldn't imagine her sister being a tomboy. There was no way.

Joy frowned. "You don't know our family, or you'd understand. We were raised to be ladylike at all times and to excel in housewifely tasks. Cooking, sewing, cleaning, and crafts. Honor hates all of that." She tilted her head to one side. "Well, she loves woodworking. Is that a craft?"

"I guess. But Grace doesn't hate all of that?"

"Nope, Grace is more like the rest of us. I'll talk to her tonight. Want me to let you know what she says?"

"If you wouldn't mind, I'd really like that." Marcus smiled. "I know that Kolby has my number. He won't mind if you call, will he?"

"Nope. He won't mind a bit." She looked at

the shopping cart and saw he'd put everything away. "Thanks for your help."

"No problem." Marcus watched her get into the car and drive away, his mind on the girl in the photo she'd shown him. Hopefully she would be as sweet as she looked.

*****

Grace was in her room, sneaking her favorite show on Netflix when her sister, Joy, called her. She wasn't allowed to watch the show, because there was too much kissing involved, but she was almost twenty-one for gosh sakes. How much could it hurt? She knew all about sex and kissing. Not that she'd ever done either.

She pressed the pause button on *Lazy Love* before answering the phone. "Hey, Joy. How's Wyoming?"

"We need you here." Joy's voice was firm.

"We've got lots of stuff on its way there. We've already started packing boxes and shipping them. Are you sure your mother-in-law can handle four of us?"

"Yes! She took all four of us in when we got there, and now we're all married off and out of her house. Time for you to invade."

"Honor loves the idea of going out there and playing cowgirl, and Patience and Felicity want to open the bakery. They're shipping stuff too. Better start watching for it." Grace paused, looking at her favorite heroine, Jo, frozen on the screen of her iPad. "We're planning on leaving on Friday. Should be there around noonish on Sunday."

"Oh, I'm so excited! I talked to Linda, and she said you guys could use the second bunkhouse for the bakery, because it has a commercial kitchen. Karlan has pulled some strings to get it inspected so you'll be ready to be up and running as soon as you get here."

"Sounds good to me. What about that lawyer you mentioned? Is he still interested in meeting me?" Grace wasn't sure how she felt about getting involved with a man as soon as she was out from under her father's roof, but Marcus sounded nice.

"Yes! I talked to him just today. He asked about you, hoping you'd be coming. Want me to invite you both to dinner on Monday?"

Grace thought about it for a moment. "No, I want to get the bakery set up first. As soon as that's done, I'll meet him happily."

"Sounds good to me! I'm so happy you're coming!"

"Me too!" Grace ended the call and pushed the play button on her iPad, sighing contentedly. Who wouldn't be happy to watch Dylan kiss Jo? The couple had a chemistry that just made her heart beat faster.

As she watched the scene she'd seen at least fifteen times before, she thought about what they still had to do to get out of the house. Grace had talked to her parents about going to stay with the sisters, and her mother had reluctantly agreed. She didn't realize they weren't coming back, but that was better than just running off as her older quadruplet sisters had done. She and Honor were at least admitting what they were doing. Well, as much as they could without their parents going ballistic.

She zoned out watching her show for a while, and then switched to watching some of the interviews of the stars on YouTube. She found one from a couple of months before where the two main stars appeared on the *Night* show right after marrying in real life.

She'd seen it before, but she still laughed and blushed when Valerie was asked very personal questions and ended up kissing her new husband, Jesse Savoy. It was too bad her sisters hadn't moved to Texas, instead of Wyoming. She'd have loved to casually drive by the set and see if she could catch a glimpse of Valerie and Jesse.

She fell asleep with a smile on her face, imagining having that kind of chemistry with a man. Someday it would happen for her. It had to.

*****

The drive to Wyoming was long and tedious. They took the car Grace and Honor's father had purchased for them when they'd begun college. All of Grace's baking pans and specialty equipment had been shipped ahead.

As they crossed the state line into Wyoming on Sunday morning, Grace found herself becoming more and more nervous. Patience and Felicity sat in the back seat singing show tunes the whole way. It made Grace more than a little crazy, but their voices weren't horrible. It was just being locked up in a car for so long that was getting to her.

When they started their fifth rendition of

"Moses Supposes His Toeses are Roses" from *Singing in the Rain*, she thought about screaming, but instead she turned to Honor. "Are you excited to be going to the ranch? I'm sure the brothers will let you help out."

Honor shrugged. "I'm more excited to finally be able ride a horse."

"I still don't understand why Mom and Dad didn't want you taking horseback riding lessons when we were kids." Grace knew Honor had begged and begged for the privilege, but her sister had never been allowed.

"Daddy would have been fine with it if I'd been willing to ride sidesaddle, but he said that riding astride wasn't something one of his daughters was going to do on his watch."

"That's stupid." Grace shook her head. "Why do they have such antiquated beliefs?"

"I have no idea." Honor rolled her eyes, turning left on a highway at the GPS system's prompting. "How much longer does it say?"

Grace looked at the screen. "Five minutes."

Patience and Felicity quit singing at her words. "Five minutes?" Felicity asked.

Patience let out a squeal. "In five minutes, we can get out of this car and wander around. I can't wait to see the quads!"

Grace frowned. She knew everyone had always found it easier to refer to her older sisters as the quads and her and Honor as the twins, but she found it annoying. They weren't who they were because they happened to have been part of multiple births. They were people in their own right.

As soon as Honor parked the car, Grace got out, stretching. "This place is huge."

Honor got out beside her, nodding emphatically. "I want to go see the stables." She took off in the direction of a building that looked like a stable, ignoring her sister and cousins.

"Honor, where are you going?" Grace yelled after her twin. "We're supposed to meet the Culpeppers!"

Grace walked toward the house, tripping over her own two feet as she did all the time. She blamed her name. Her parents hadn't realized that giving her a name like Grace was just asking for her to be clumsy. Just like Chastity did everything she could to live down to her name, Grace found herself living down to her own—without intending to.

A woman who appeared to be in her late forties came out of the house, wearing a pair of jeans and a button-up shirt. "Hello!" she called out. "Are you Grace?"

Grace nodded, walking toward Linda Culpepper, their hostess. "Thank you for inviting us to stay for a while."

Linda enfolded Grace in a hug. "We're just happy you're all willing to come and help us out of our jam."

"Family helps family. Joy said you were able to find a place for us to set up a bakery?" Grace was so excited to be able to use her skills. Back in Kentucky, she'd frequently made cakes and cupcakes for friends and family for birthdays and weddings, but she'd never been able to start a business using them, because their parents didn't think girls should work.

"Yes, we do. We have a second bunkhouse that hasn't been used in about ten years, but the kitchen is a commercial kitchen. My father-in-law sold off part of the ranch ten years ago, so we didn't need as many men to run it. That's about the time the boys were finishing up their schooling, and now it's a family business only, if you don't count Angus."

"Angus works for you, right?" Grace asked, not having heard the name from her sisters.

"He's our only employee. He's a good man." Linda led the three women into the house. "Who's missing? I thought I was getting four young ladies."

"Honor went to check out the horses," Grace responded. "She's always been horse crazy."

"Oh, so she rides?"

Grace shook her head. "Not yet. I'm sure it's only a matter of time, though."

Linda didn't ask any questions, obviously used to the crazy way the Quinlan girls had been raised. "Come on in. You'll each have your own room here in what we call the big house. I'm going to text your sisters to let them know you got here a little earlier than expected."

"That would be great. Thank you." She quickly introduced her cousins, and they made their way down the hall, with Linda assigning a room to each of them. "I'm going to throw some lunch together. You girls come out when you're ready.

Tomorrow morning, I'll show you the bakery."

Grace took the first room to the right, sighing in relief once she was inside. It had a private bathroom, which thrilled her to no end. She quickly stripped and showered, not wanting to see her sisters when she was so unkempt after a two-month absence. Of the six Quinlan sisters, Grace was known to be the most obsessed with her appearance.

She dressed in jeans and a T-shirt, before walking out into her bedroom. There was a sharp knock on her door, and then it was thrown open. "Joy!"

Grace ran into her sister's arms. For some reason, she'd always felt closer to Joy than she had any of the others, except Honor, of course.

Joy grabbed her in a bear hug. "I'm so glad you're here!"

"How are you feeling? How's my little niece or nephew?"

Joy smiled. "Morning sickness is going to be the death of me. I can't believe I have six more weeks of this to look forward to."

Grace frowned. "You're not due in six weeks."

"No, but the doctor said it won't be this bad after the first trimester, and that's another six weeks."

"Well, I'm excited about the baby." Grace peered at her sister's stomach, trying to see if she was showing at all, but she couldn't see anything.

"No, I'm not showing yet," Joy said with a frown. "Of course, as a newlywed, I don't want to be huge, but I do want this baby with everything in me."

"I can't believe you and Faith both got pregnant so quick!"

"Oh, you'll understand once you meet our husbands. These Culpepper men are—well, I heard Dr. Lachele tell Linda that her boys are all 'sex on a stick.' And they are."

Grace grinned at that. "I'm sorry Dr. Lachele isn't here so we could meet her." She'd wanted to meet the older woman since she'd heard about Dr. Lachele's first meeting with her older sisters a few months before.

Joy shrugged. "Oh, she visits regularly. You'll see her."

"Why? Does she do that with all the couples she matches?"

"I don't think so, but she and Linda have become really close." Joy grabbed Grace's arm and pulled her from the room. "We need to go help with lunch. Linda is left with the burden of cooking for the entire horde too often."

Grace happily joined her sister, going into the kitchen. Hope, Chastity, and Faith were all there, talking to Linda. Grace squealed when she saw her sisters, feeling like it had been years. She'd talked to Joy regularly but not to any of the others.

Hope was the first to spot Grace, and she opened her arms. Grace flew to her like she'd been called home, surprising herself with tears. "I've missed y'all so much! It was so hard at home without you four."

Hope hugged her sister close. "It was hard leaving you. I'm glad you joined us here."

Their reunion was cut short by the back door opening. Four tall men walked into the house, stopping a few feet away from where she stood. One of them looked at Grace. "Didn't I just see you outside poking around the stables? You were wearing something different."

Grace grinned. "That was my twin sister, Honor."

"Wait, you two are identical?"

Joy walked to the man and stood on tiptoe to kiss his cheek. "This very rude man is my husband, Kolby."

Grace just grinned. "We aren't identical, but if we dressed alike you'd have trouble telling us apart. We have the same coloring and the same facial features. Our eyes are identical. There are little ways to tell us apart, though, if you know them. As it is, you'll have no trouble. Honor will always be the one in jeans and a cowboy hat. I usually wear dresses." She didn't add that her sister never fixed her hair or wore make-up. Why point out the obvious?

All four of the men frowned at her. "How come no one told us you two looked so much alike?" another of them asked.

Hope moved to the man who'd asked the second question. "This one is my Karlan."

"Maybe someone could just introduce all four of them and get it over with to make it easier?" Grace asked.

Faith laughed. "Well, you know those two. This is Cooper, and he's mine. And that one draped all over Chastity is her husband, Chris. Though they didn't let us see the wedding, so we just have to take their word for it."

"Thank you, Faith." Grace let her eyes move from one brother-in-law to the other, trying to remember who was whom. "It's nice to meet all of you."

The doorbell rang then, and Linda dried off her hands and headed to the door. "Y'all just keep talking. I'll be right back."

Grace looked at Hope and Karlan, who were holding hands. "So when do I get to see my new bakery?"

"Mom said she wants to take you over tomorrow. I've had it inspected, and your sisters gave it a good cleaning. I've started the process of getting you ladies licensed as well, and that should be completed by Wednesday. You'll be up and running by the end of the week," Karlan informed her.

Grace's eyes widened with surprise. "I had no idea you'd been doing all that!"

Hope grinned. "Well, we want you to be able to make money to help out, and we knew that's what you needed. Karlan's the mayor of Culpepper, so he pulled a few strings."

Linda came to them then with a man beside her. He'd obviously just come from church, and was wearing a suit with a cowboy hat. He removed the hat. "Excuse me. I didn't realize I'd be interrupting a big party."

Joy smiled at him. "You're not interrupting, Marcus."

"I brought the will back to you," Marcus said to Karlan. "Sorry I wasn't able to find a way out of your predicament, but there just isn't one."

Karlan took the will, frowning. "I didn't think we'd find anything, but I appreciate you looking into it for us."

Linda smiled at the newcomer. "Why don't you stay for lunch? I cooked a lot, because the girls just got here from Kentucky."

Marcus looked around the room, only seeing one girl he hadn't already met. "I'm Marcus Wells."

"Nice to meet you," Grace said with a smile, immediately knowing this was the man Joy wanted her to meet. "What do you call forty lawyers at the bottom of the ocean?"

Marcus's eyes narrowed. Was this the girl Joy had wanted him to meet? She was telling him lawyer jokes within seconds of meeting him? "I don't know."

"A good start." Grace stifled a giggle. "I'm Grace by the way."

"I had a feeling you were. Is the urge to tell lawyer jokes out of your system now?" She was beautiful. She couldn't be an inch over five feet, and she had blond hair and the biggest blue eyes he'd ever seen. He wanted to ask her to go to dinner with him right away, but thought it might be too much considering they'd just met.

"For the moment." She smiled, crooking her

finger at him, so he leaned down. "I never run out of lawyer jokes, though."

Marcus wanted to groan. "Great."

Grace was surprised at the tall, handsome cowboy beside her. She'd expected someone who looked like he sat behind a desk all day and really hadn't been looking forward to meeting the man. Instead, she saw a man who obviously did some kind of physical work or at least spent a lot of time in a gym.

"Maybe we could take a walk after lunch?" Marcus asked, wanting to get to know her better. "I've heard a lot about you from Joy."

Grace nodded. "We could do that. Do you mean walk here on the ranch? Or somewhere else?" She could see mountains out the window, and she desperately wanted to get closer, but she wasn't sure she was up to it after the long trip. She was tired.

"Oh, just here on the ranch today. I'll show you around Culpepper soon if I don't run screaming from your lawyer jokes."

"No one runs screaming from my lawyer jokes," she said with a wink.

Joy was grinning between the two of them. "His grandfather is Brother Anthony, the man who married all of us."

Grace grinned, remembering what her sister had told her about the pastor. "Oh, I can't *wait* to meet him!"

"Grandpa is interesting, all right." Marcus shook his head.

Grace saw Patience and Felicity approaching,

both fresh from showers. "Marcus, these are my cousins, Patience and Felicity. They're here to run the bakery with me."

Marcus nodded politely, tipping his hat at both of them. "Nice to meet you, ladies." They were pretty enough, but for some reason, he was drawn to Grace in a way that surprised him. He didn't know if it was because Joy had suggested he take her to dinner once she arrived, and he'd been anticipating her arrival, or if he truly wasn't as attracted to them.

Lunch proved to be a boisterous affair. Honor never did make an appearance, but Grace didn't worry about her. She knew her sister was content in the middle of the smelly stable.

"What's the difference between an accountant and a lawyer?" Grace asked, taking a big bite of her potato salad.

Marcus frowned at her. "This is going to happen on a regular basis, isn't it?"

"An accountant knows he's boring." Grace nudged his foot with hers under the table, hoping he'd know she was teasing him.

Marcus rolled his eyes as the four Culpepper men roared with laughter. "I like your sister," Cooper said to Faith.

"She's always had this thing for lawyer jokes. Seriously, I think she was like fifteen and she got a book of lawyer jokes. I don't know why they amused her so much, but she's been telling them for years," Faith responded.

Marcus sighed. "So if I ask you out, I need to just expect lawyer jokes?"

Grace nodded, her eyes lit with laughter. "They *are* kind of my thing."

"Duly noted." Marcus could see the way the Culpepper brothers were studying him interestedly. "What?" he finally asked.

Karlan shrugged. "She's family now. I guess we're trying to figure out if you're worthy of walking with her after lunch."

Grace's eyes widened. "I had enough of that at home. I can go right back there if you men are going to start it here, because I'm my own woman, and I'll walk with a skunk after lunch if that's what I want to do."

Karlan held his hands up. "I'm just trying to watch out for my kid sister."

"Stop." Grace wasn't going to allow herself to be smothered ever again. She'd come to Wyoming for the opportunity to start her own business and stand on her own two feet. She didn't care if the four big galoots did think they were supposed to take care of her. Taking care of herself was her first priority.

Marcus eyed her with a grin. He leaned close. "Good answer!"

She raised an eyebrow at him, letting him know she wouldn't put up with nonsense from him either. "I'm a strong woman. I'll prove it if it's the last thing I do." Grace needed to prove her strength as much as her sister Honor did, but she knew they'd go about it in different ways. Grace would want to prove herself strong of character. Honor wanted to prove she could do a man's job, and do it as well as he could.

Grace had never felt the need to prove herself that way. Thank heavens.

Chapter Two

As soon as lunch was over, Grace stood to help with clearing the table. Faith shook her head at her. "You four are excused from household chores today. Settle in."

Marcus stood beside the back door, watching her. "You ready?"

Grace nodded. "Are these shoes okay? How far are we going?" She looked down at the sandals she wore. They'd be fine as long as they weren't walking miles and miles.

"Um…I'd like to walk for an hour or so. Will they work?" Marcus asked. He wanted time to get to know her, and he didn't want to have to cut their walk short because of her shoes when she could easily change before they left.

"Let me go put some tennis shoes on." She hurried to the small room she was using and took off her sandals and exchanged them for socks and tennis shoes. Hurrying back into the dining room, she saw that Karlan was talking to Marcus.

"No matter what she says, she's our sister now, and you'd better treat her right." Karlan's words floated across the room to her as she walked back to Marcus.

"Karlan? You are my new brother, but I met

you less than two hours ago. You will back off, and you will be nice about it." She stepped up to Marcus and smiled. "I'm ready."

Marcus winked at Joy, who was watching carefully, before leading her sister out the back door. "So, tell me about Kentucky. I want to hear everything."

"Oh, there's not a lot to tell. We grew up in a tiny little town near Paducah. Everyone knew everyone, and my sisters and I were a bit of a novelty, because of the multiple thing, and because our parents were so strict."

"They were strict?" Marcus asked, not having heard any of the story.

"Very. I've never dated anyone in my life. Our father wouldn't allow it. In fact, we were allowed to go to college, but we were only allowed to major in homemaking. Honor and I quit after our freshman year."

"So what did you do back in Kentucky?"

Grace laughed. "Do? Why I made cakes for people for their birthdays and for weddings. And I sneaked into my room every chance I got and watched my favorite television show."

"Why did you have to sneak into your room to watch television?"

"Because there was kissing on it. People aren't supposed to kiss before they get married, you know."

Marcus blinked at her a couple of times before laughing. "You're joking, right?"

She shook her head. "Unfortunately, no. My

parents were very strict in what we were allowed to watch. Mainly things like *I Love Lucy*."

"I see," he said, but he didn't. Not really. She was an adult. She should be able to watch whatever she wanted. "What show did you watch?"

"*Lazy Love*."

The way she said it told him a whole lot about how she felt about the show. There was a bit of a sigh in her voice as if she was absolutely mesmerized by it. "I haven't seen it."

"Really? Oh, it's wonderful! It's about a girl who was raised by her rich father after her mother died. He had no idea what to do with her, so he sent her off to boarding school, and then to this really ritzy prestigious college. When he died, she had a seventeen-year-old sister to take care of and she had no idea how to do it. She inherited his ranch and had to run it. And then she fell for her veterinarian, but she wouldn't marry him right off, because she needed to learn to stand on her own two feet." She identified with Jo more than she'd admit.

"Sounds like it could be interesting."

"I think they'll have them marry in the season finale. The two main characters just got married in real life, and she's already pregnant, so they'll have to address that."

"You follow the real life stars?"

"Oh, did I say I watch the show? I mean, I'm addicted to the show. I watch all their interviews. I search the internet for pictures of them together. I watch every episode over and over until I have it memorized."

He blinked a couple of times. "Well, it sounds like something you enjoy."

"Seriously. The couple that's on it together is incredible. You watch one of their kissing scenes, and it's like the entire room they're in is on fire. You can almost see them spontaneously combust!"

"But you don't believe in kissing before marriage!"

She laughed softly, looking at him out of the corner of her eye. "My parents don't believe in kissing before marriage. Chastity had her first kiss under a table in Sunday School when the quads were two."

"And you? When was your first kiss?" Marcus watched her carefully. He had planned to take her somewhere isolated and kiss her. See if there was anything between them. Now it looked like that might be out of the question.

"Oh, I'm afraid I was a good little girl. I've never had a boyfriend and never been kissed. So boring." Grace shrugged, trying to laugh it off. She couldn't though. She felt like she was defective sometimes.

"So are you opposed to kissing before marriage, or no? Are you willing to watch it on television only? Or could I grab you and kiss you right now?"

Grace grinned at him. "Are we out of eyesight of the house?"

Marcus looked over his shoulder. They'd been walking a straight line away from the main house on the Culpepper ranch. "I think we're far enough away."

"Then let's walk for another five minutes to be sure." She felt her heart start beating faster as they walked, knowing he'd be kissing her soon. What it was about him that made her want to dive into his arms, she didn't know.

"So that means you want to kiss me?"

She smiled. "It means I'm attracted to you, and willing to give it a try."

He laughed. "I like your honesty. Thanks for not playing games."

"I wouldn't know how to play games. I've lived my life in a protective bubble that all but suffocated me." She frowned, not wanting to continue that line of conversation. "What's the difference between a vacuum cleaner and a lawyer on a motorcycle?"

He thought he understood her game then. Anytime she became uncomfortable, she'd tell him a lawyer joke. She was an odd woman, but if it made her feel better, he'd play along. "I don't know. What?"

"The vacuum cleaner has the dirt bag on the inside."

He grinned, reaching out and capturing her hand. "How many of these jokes do you have?"

She shrugged, feeling electricity shoot through her body as his fingers intertwined with hers. "Oh, an endless supply."

He took them a little further to an isolated wooded area. He knew they were still on the Culpepper Ranch, but he knew there was little chance they would be spotted there. "May I kiss you?" he asked softly, his eyes on hers.

She stared up into his big brown eyes, her eyes memorizing every feature of his face, wanting to always remember how he'd looked at her the first time he kissed her. Nodding, she put her free hand onto his shoulder, frowning at how high she had to reach up.

"Why the frown?" he asked softly, not wanting to do something she didn't want him to do.

"You're so much bigger than me. I feel like a tiny little porcelain doll. Like the kind Faith makes."

He knew nothing about the kind of dolls Faith made, but if she wasn't frowning at the idea of kissing him, then he was going to go for it. He leaned down and gently pressed his lips to hers, his free hand cupping her face.

As soon as Grace felt his lips on hers, she felt as if something inside her that had lain dormant came alive for the first time. She took a step closer to him, wanting to feel his body against hers. She felt like her favorite character, Jo, looked after she was kissed by Dylan.

She pulled away for a moment to look up into his eyes. "And now I understand why my daddy didn't want me kissing boys before I married." She stood on tiptoe, her body pressed against his as she pulled his head down for another kiss.

Marcus felt as if his head was spinning. This tiny little woman was making him feel more than he'd imagined he could from a simple kiss. Finally, after a minute, he pulled away. "I think we're compatible."

She laughed. "I have this feeling you're right. Wow."

"Wow?"

"Yeah. That's all. Just wow."

He slipped his arm around her shoulders to continue their walk, knowing he wouldn't be as tempted to grab her for another kiss if they were moving. "So does that mean kissing is all you'd thought it would be?"

"Let's just say you could give Dr. Dylan Drake a run for his money."

"And who is Dr. Dylan Drake?" She'd lost him, and he had a feeling it wouldn't be the last time.

"He's the veterinarian the main character on my show is in love with." She sighed. "You know, the one who she kisses and the entire house is suddenly on fire, and no one even notices, because that's how hot their kisses are?"

"I'm going to have to watch that show!" Even if it wasn't his kind of show, at least he'd understand her a little bit better.

"I'd love to watch it with you." As soon as the words were out of her mouth, she was a bit worried. Would he think it was an invitation to make out with her, because they were watching the stars of the show kiss?

"I'd love that!" He grinned at her, continuing their walk, but not telling her where he was taking her. The small ranch he owned was just on the other side of the Culpeppers' and they should be able to get there in another thirty minutes or so. He'd left his truck, but they could take his motorcycle back, and he could bring that home in his truck bed. Besides, he wasn't dressed for walking. He wanted to get into jeans and a comfortable shirt.

"Shouldn't we turn back?" she asked.

He shook his head. "No, I want to show you something, and it's just a bit further."

"All right."

"You're not going to ask what I want to show you?" he asked, surprised.

She shrugged. "I trust you. Joy said you were a good guy."

"And you trust your sister." Marcus was able to just see his house beyond the trees. There was a fence dividing the properties, but he had climbed through it many times. Never in a suit, but they could do it. He walked to the fence and held the barbed wire apart. "After you!"

"Are we allowed to go there?" she asked, surprised.

He nodded. "That's my property. It's fine."

She shrugged and climbed between the wires on the fence, before carefully taking them to hold them apart for him. "Wait! Give me your jacket."

He nodded, taking off his suit coat and handing it to her. She looked at the fence and then at the coat in her hands before shrugging it on, before pushing the sleeves up to her elbows so she wouldn't snag them when she held the wires of the fence apart for him again.

He quickly climbed through the fence, and

waited for her to offer his coat back, but when she didn't, he shrugged.

Grace took his hand again, not needing his coat for warmth, but liking the feel of it fresh from his skin. It felt cozy, and it smelled like he did.

"Why are we going to your house?" she asked, walking in the direction of the big white house in front of them.

"Because I took you so far, we were closer to my house than the Culpeppers'. Thought it might be nice to show you around, and I'll take you home on my motorcycle. I can put it in the bed of the truck and drive it back."

"Motorcycle?" Grace asked, her eyes wide. Her parents had always been dead set against motorcycles, so naturally she was fascinated by them.

He nodded. "Do you mind?"

She shook her head, loving the idea. "I'd like to see your house too. Make sure you're a good housekeeper and all that."

He laughed. "I don't keep my own house. One of my grandmother's best friends, Ethel, lost her husband a few years back, and she had no way to support herself, so I offered her a job as my housekeeper and cook."

"Oh." Grace wasn't sure if she was relieved or disappointed he had a housekeeper. "Does she live in?"

He nodded. "She's probably out right now, but she lives in. She usually spends Sunday afternoons with her grandkids."

Her heart beat a bit faster at his words. She would be totally alone with a man she'd just met hours before. If her parents could see her, they'd shoot her, but they were in Kentucky, and she was in Wyoming. They certainly couldn't reach that far.

"Will it bother you to be alone with me?" he asked. "I didn't think it was different than being in the woods together, but if it bothers you, just tell me, and I'll go in and change and take you back."

Grace shook her head. "It would bother my parents a lot, but it doesn't bother me."

"Good." He smiled at her for a moment, stopping walking. "I really want you to see my place."

"Why?"

He shrugged. "I'm not sure. I guess I want our relationship to be able to move quickly."

She frowned. "How quickly? I'm okay with kissing before marriage, but not more than that."

"I gathered that. I won't press for anything more before marriage. I promise."

"I appreciate that." He walked to the front door and opened it wide, letting her precede him into the house. "I didn't know you were going to already be at the ranch today. I hope you didn't think I came over to force a meeting before you were ready."

She shook her head. "Not at all. I'm glad we met as soon as I got to town. I'm very glad to meet you."

"And kiss me?"

"Even gladder to do that." She frowned for a

moment. "Is gladder a word?"

"I'm not sure. I like it, though, so even if it's not, we'll pretend it is!" He leaned down to kiss her softly. "I'm going to run upstairs to my room to change into jeans, and then I'll show you around. I need to get out of this suit."

She nodded, shrugging his coat off. She wanted to keep his smell on her for a little longer, but she didn't want to be so obvious about it. "Thanks for the loan."

"No problem." He looked at her. "Are you cold? I could get you something warmer to wear."

She shook her head. "No, I'm fine."

When she didn't explain why she'd kept the jacket, he shrugged and took the stairs two at a time to go change.

Chapter Three

Grace watched Marcus go, before wandering over to the couch and sitting down. She'd get her fix while she waited for him, immediately pulling up Twitter on her phone and looking at the Lazy Love hashtag to see what everyone had been saying about the show. She never used Twitter except for looking at what the stars had posted and what the fans were predicting.

She giggled as she read one of the writers saying that he was going to explode the ranch house with everyone in it and send in a giant radioactive piece of bacon to kill off all the characters who lived there. The writers were always trying to mess with the fans' heads, but she didn't believe one word of their nonsense.

She saw some of the other fans going crazy with all kinds of crazy emoticons and just kept giggling. And then she saw a link to a short video she'd watched once before, but she had to watch again. She clicked on it and watched Valerie and Jesse Savoy excitedly admit that she was expecting their first child.

She had been impressed to hear that Valerie was taking his name. When she'd tweeted her to ask about it, the response had been special. *I know I'll* never divorce, so taking his name seems like the right thing to do. Besides, I love him, and I want his name. #lazylove

One of her favorite things about the show was how available the stars and writers were. It warmed her heart. She was just going back to Twitter from the announcement when she heard Marcus coming down the stairs. She looked up at him, her eyes bright with tears.

He hurried to her, taking her hand in his. "Are you okay? Bad news from someone?"

She shook her head. "No, I was just rewatching a video where the stars from my favorite show announced they're expecting their first child."

"So you've seen it before, and it still makes you cry?"

She nodded. "It does. I know I'm a dork, but that's how I roll. All right?"

"Sure. Whatever makes you happy!" He liked the fact that she seemed so tenderhearted. "Want to see the house?"

She nodded. "I'd like that."

"I grew up here," he explained as he took her through the downstairs first. "My parents decided to take a job in Florida, because Mom does better in a warmer climate, so they left me the house and the ranch. I was done with law school when they decided to leave, so I hired a foreman to run things around here. I love this place, and want to leave it to my children, but I'm not terribly interested in the day to day running of the place."

She nodded, looking at everything. "You want

kids?"

He shrugged. "Eventually. I probably don't want them next week. I want to have a year or two alone with my wife before any little knee biters come along." His eyes met hers. "You?"

"The same. I want the bakery up and running before I need to start thinking about morning sickness and diapers."

He continued leading her through the house. "Ethel lives in a room off the kitchen. I told her to pick any room she wanted, but she said that was the one she belonged in. At least she has a private bathroom." He'd have given her the master bedroom if she'd asked.

He led her into the kitchen and she smiled at all the cool gadgets. "This would be fun to cook in."

"Do you like to cook?"

She laughed. "I prefer to bake, but I'm a good cook. We may end up adding catering to the business before all is said and done. Who knows?"

He nodded, leading her to the stairs. "My office and bedroom are upstairs. There are three spare rooms as well."

"This place is huge."

"Before the economic downturn here in Wyoming, we had a lot of ranch hands. There are fewer now, but it still takes a lot of men to run a ranch. My mom thought she'd have at least a dozen kids, but her health has never been good. She only had me."

"That's sad. I think if women want lots of kids, they should be able to have them."

"If only life really worked that way." Marcus led her into his office, showing her around. "I do work from home a couple of days a week. I run my own practice so no one really cares."

"That reminds me. What's the difference between a lawyer and a jellyfish?"

He shook his head at her. "If these keep going, I'm going to start kissing you just to shut you up."

"One's a spineless, poisonous blob. The other is a form of sea life."

He shook his head. "You deserve a penalty for that one."

"What kind of penalty?" She didn't really care what he said, of course. She loved her lawyer jokes, and dating a lawyer, as it appeared she was doing, was going to make them so much more fun.

"I'm not sure. I'll think it through."

"Well, when you decide let me know, and I'll let you know if I accept the penalty."

He sighed. "You're a sassy little thing, aren't you?"

"At least I'm not hiding my true nature. You're being forewarned!"

"It's a good thing you're so pretty. I might have to make you walk home otherwise."

She shrugged. "You could. It wouldn't hurt me a bit."

"You're supposed to shriek and act like it would kill you if I forced you to walk home."

"I am?" She sighed dramatically. "I'll never get the hang of all this man-woman stuff. Maybe you should give me up as a lost cause."

"Why don't you think you'll ever get the hang of it?"

"Because I refuse to be someone I'm not. Men don't seem to like honesty, just subterfuge."

He laughed. "I like you. You know that?"

"Good, because you're kind of growing on me."

He sighed. "Let's get you home. It'll be dark soon, and I don't need Linda Culpepper coming to find you."

"She just met me this morning. She wouldn't come looking for me. My sisters might, but she wouldn't."

He shook his head. "You just met her this morning, but I've known her my whole life. She would come find you. I promise." Linda took care of those she considered her own. Grace would be one of hers.

"I'll take your word for it."

He led her through the house and down to his garage, which was off the kitchen. "Let me find you a helmet."

While he was looking, she watched him, smiling to herself. He was a good man. She could be happy with him. "Can I make a request before you take me back to Linda's house?"

"Sure. Whatever you want." He found the helmet and held it up, carrying it over to her.

"Will you kiss me again? I want to make sure I didn't imagine how it felt."

He raised an eyebrow, a grin turning up one

corner of his lips. "How did it feel?"

"Like magic fairy dust was sprinkled all over my body, starting from my lips and traveling all the way to my toes. I think I like kissing."

He stared at her in disbelief. She really did have no experience with men, or she wouldn't have admitted that and given him so much power over her. "Magic fairy dust, huh?"

She nodded. "Think you can make it happen again?"

"I'm sure I can." He caught her about her waist and pulled her to him, holding her against his body.

She wrapped her arms around his neck and lifted her lips to his. As soon as his lips touched hers again, the magic began. She'd never felt anything quite like it. She parted her lips for his, and she felt his tongue stroke the inside of her upper lip.

She moaned softly. "I wonder if it'd be like this if I kissed someone else."

He frowned at her. "I'd rather you didn't run around trying to find out."

She grinned. "I can't really see myself doing that. I like kissing you. I think you bring the magic. I don't think a random man off the street could do it."

"You just keep thinking that, and we'll be just fine!" He grabbed his helmet and put it on, while she strapped hers on. "What are you doing tomorrow?"

"All of our baking supplies were shipped, and Linda said they've been putting them into the bakery. So we'll probably spend tomorrow setting it up."

"Will you and your twin and both cousins all work there?"

Grace laughed. "Honor wouldn't do it if we paid her. She wanted to come, but only so she could try to work on the ranch with the men. Do you think they'll let her?"

He made a face. "I don't know. The Culpeppers tend to be pretty traditional. They might surprise me, though."

"Honor would never be happy being cooped up inside all day. She loves being outdoors. When we were little, we'd have a picnic under this tree in our backyard. All four of our older sisters and I would be sitting there quietly, doing whatever craft we'd brought along, and Honor would be dangling from the highest branch at the top of the tree."

He smiled at the idea. "I can't wait to meet her."

Grace laughed. "We're actually fraternal twins, but we look so alike, and act so differently, that we confuse everyone."

"Okay." He'd just go with that. He threw a leg over the motorcycle and waited for her to climb on behind him before starting it. Her arms wrapped tightly around his waist, and he realized then that he was going to make her his wife. Feeling her arms around him was like coming in from a week in the snow and being surrounded by warmth while sipping on hot chocolate.

Grace rested her cheek against his shoulder, giggling as he took off out of his driveway. She liked his motorcycle. More than she probably should.

When he stopped the cycle in front of Linda's house and got off, she was disappointed their time together was over. "When will I see you again?" she asked.

He grinned. "Well, you said you were working all day tomorrow."

"I have to eat." She knew her mother would be appalled at the way she was angling for an invitation, but she didn't care. She wanted to see him again soon.

"You do." He tapped her nose with his finger. "Why don't I come get you around six, and you can have dinner with me at my place? And maybe you can introduce me to that show of yours tomorrow evening."

She grinned at his words. Not only would she have time with Marcus, but she could introduce him to Jo and Dylan. "What do you throw a drowning lawyer?" she asked, needing to end the special day with one of her favorite jokes.

He sighed. "This is really going to keep happening, isn't it?"

"Oh, yeah!" She waited and when he didn't answer, she said, "His partners!"

He groaned, leaning down to kiss her softly. "Tomorrow evening. Wear something comfortable."

She nodded, stroking his cheek with her hand. "I think I'm going to keep you."

"Oh, you are, are you?"

Grace smiled, turning to hurry into the house. Of course she was going to keep him. He was the nicest lawyer she'd ever met.

Linda was in the kitchen when she got back. "You took longer than I expected. I was starting to get worried!"

"Oh, I'm fine, Mrs. Culpepper. Marcus took me for a walk over to his house, and then he brought me back on his motorcycle." Grace smiled dreamily as she thought about sitting on the back of the cycle with her arms wrapped tightly around Marcus's waist. "It was fun!"

"Call me Linda, or even Wiggie. That's what the grandkids will call me." She turned back to the pizza she was pulling from the oven. "Did Marcus think to feed you?"

Grace shook her head. "No, but we're having dinner together tomorrow night. He's picking me up around six."

"I'm glad you two are getting along so well. Maybe you'll end up settling down here in Culpepper too." Linda cut the frozen pizza she'd just removed with a pair of scissors like it was a normal thing to do. "Do you want some?"

"Do you always cut pizza with scissors? I've never seen anyone do that before."

Linda shrugged. "I think it's a lot easier than a pizza cutter."

"All right. Yeah, pizza sounds good. Do you want me to set the table?"

Linda gestured to some paper plates on the counter. "What do you want to drink?"

"Oh, iced tea?" Grace had no idea what Linda kept around yet. She'd spent very little time in the home since her arrival.

"Sweet or unsweet?"

"Unsweet, thanks."

She took the plates from Linda after she'd piled the pizza on them and carried them to the table. "Where are the others?"

"Honor went to have dinner with Hope and Karlan. Felicity and Patience are eating with Faith and Cooper."

"I see. Did it bother you being abandoned the day we arrived?"

Linda shook her head. "Of course not. I don't feel abandoned at all. I was invited to go eat with Honor, but I wanted to wait here for you. I wanted to make sure you were all right."

"I'm sorry I worried you. I really was having a good time, and it never occurred to me you'd be worried."

Linda shrugged. "I'm a worrier. If there's ever a storm, I'll be calling to make sure you're all right."

Grace nodded. "I appreciate you looking out for all of us."

"I know you and Honor aren't my new daughters-in-law like your sisters are, but I feel like you're family anyway. You're going to have to put up with that from me."

"I can see that." Grace took a bite of her pizza, feeling slightly awkward. "We appreciate you letting us all stay here."

"It's nice to have people around. The girls and the daycare keep me smiling. And the prospect of being a Wiggie, of course."

"A Wiggie?"

"That's the name I'm going to have the grandkids call me. All fifty-seven of them."

Grace's eyes widened. "Fifty-seven? From four girls?"

Linda shrugged. "Well, I'll adopt you and Honor, of course, and I'm sure Felicity and Patience."

Grace nodded. "That's still only eight girls. That would be more than seven kids each."

"That's not too much to ask, is it?" Linda winked at Grace to let her know she was joking. At least that's what Grace hoped it meant.

"I guess not..."

Linda laughed. "I'm kidding. Mostly." She got up and cleared the table.

Grace watched her as she ate the last bite. "You cooked. You should leave the dishes for me."

Linda shook her head. "No, I'll do them. You just got here and then you spent all day wandering around. You can help tomorrow."

"I'm really excited to get to spend time organizing the bakery tomorrow. Thanks for helping make my dreams come true."

"You girls will be helping us a lot with that bakery. We appreciate the time going into it."

"The arrangement Hope made with us was more than generous." They would work until the men's deadline free of charge, and in exchange, they would be able to work out of the bunkhouse's kitchen free of charge for five years as they built up their business.

"As long as you're satisfied with it, I'm sure it will work out well." Linda turned to Grace from the dishwasher she'd been loading. "I almost forgot. A friend's daughter is having a baby. The shower is on Saturday. We were hoping you would be willing to bake the cake."

"I'd love to!"

"Oh, good, because I told her you would." Linda turned back to loading the dishwasher, missing the amused look on Grace's face.

Grace stood and stretched, taking her plate and throwing it away. "I think I'm going to go and vegetate before I fall asleep."

Linda looked at her with a smile. "What kind of vegetating?"

"That reminds me! Do you have a Wi-Fi password?"

"Yes, of course."

"I need it if you don't mind. I'll rewatch old episodes of my favorite show. It makes me happy."

"What show do you watch?" Linda asked.

"*Lazy Love*." Grace took the paper Linda handed her. "I'll be right back with it. I need to key it into my iPad." She hurried into her room and set up the Wi-Fi before returning the paper to Linda. "I'll see you in the morning."

"We usually have breakfast before the kids start coming around six-thirty," Linda informed her.

"Do you want me to cook?"

Linda shook her head. "No, you'll be working all day. There's no need."

Grace smiled. "Thank you so much. I feel like I've moved to a luxury resort. We Quinlan girls are used to doing for ourselves."

"I know you are. That's why I like to make it special for you when you come here." Linda hugged Grace tightly. "I'm glad you're here. Now go vegetate with your show."

"G'night!"

"Sleep sweet."

Grace smiled as she walked away. She'd never heard anyone use that phrase before, but she really liked it. *Sleep sweet.* She might just have to adopt that.

She wandered into her new room and changed into her pajamas. After she'd brushed her teeth, she settled into bed with her iPad, bringing up the first episode of *Lazy Love*. New life for her, so what better time to start over at the beginning with the show she loved. She sighed happily. She was going to love Wyoming.

Before long she was lost in the storyline, giggling at the stupid things Jo did as a newcomer to the ranch, and sighing over her chemistry with Dr. Dylan Drake.

When she slept that night, she didn't dream about Dr. Drake, though. No, it was a dark-haired lawyer who had captured her attention filling her dreams that night.

Chapter Four

Linda led Grace, Patience, and Felicity into the old bunkhouse an hour later. "We brought all of your boxes over, but we didn't unpack them. We thought you'd want to do that yourself."

"Thank you for making sure they got here," Grace said, speaking for all of them. Her cousins were sweet, but they tended to prefer if other people did the talking for them. You'll have to tell us where the nearest warehouse store is. We'll need to go and stock up on flour and sugar, as well as the millions of other things we'll need."

Linda smiled. "I'm going to leave you girls to it. I'll find the location of the nearest store, but it's going to be a drive."

Grace shrugged. "As long as we have today out of the car, we'll be able to manage driving again tomorrow. We may not like it, but we're tough."

"Let me know if you need me." Linda left to go back to help with the daycare.

Grace looked around the kitchen. There were two huge commercial size ovens and a separate six burner stove. A walk-in freezer and a separate walk-in refrigerator, and a long stainless steel table filled the room. "I think this is going to work."

Patience wandered around, opening every

drawer. "There's nothing left here, so it's just what we brought with us."

Felicity nodded. "But we brought and sent ahead a ton of stuff. We'll be able to work for a while without buying any new supplies as long as we have our ingredients."

Grace took one of the boxes and started unpacking it. "I think we should sanitize everything after shipping it, so let's get started."

Felicity wrinkled her nose. "I know you're right, but I sure don't want you to be."

"What we want and what we get are frequently different. I'd like the kitchen set up by late afternoon, so I can get ready for my date this evening."

Patience grinned at Grace. "You like the lawyer?"

Grace grinned, a far-away look on her face. "I do. He's a nice man and a good sport."

"How many lawyer jokes did you tell him?" Felicity asked as she opened the huge dishwasher and started loading things the other two were removing from the boxes.

"Oh, not more than ten," Grace said, giggling softly.

Patience shook her head. "Only you, Grace."

*****

By the time Marcus arrived that evening, Grace had showered for the second time that day and had her long blond hair styled and hanging around her shoulders. Her make-up was done to perfection, and she was wearing a loose skirt and a nice blouse. It was her first real date, and she was excited.

Marcus came to the door, and Grace opened it, her eyes traveling up and down his body. He was wearing a pair of tight jeans and a button-up shirt. He was holding a motorcycle helmet in each hand.

Grace took the helmet from him, grinning. "I love your motorcycle." She wasn't sure if she loved it because it was fun, or because she knew her parents would have a fit if they knew about it? As rebellions went, it was a small one for an almost twenty-one-year-old, but it made her so happy.

He smiled. "Do you want to go for a ride before we go to my house?"

She debated for only a moment. "Yes, if you don't mind."

He shook his head. "I'll take you closer to the mountains. No use living in the most beautiful place on earth if you never get close enough to see what makes it so special."

She frowned for a moment. There were no pockets in her skirt, and she didn't want to have to take her purse on his motorcycle, so she carefully tucked her phone into her bra, so she'd have it if she needed it.

He gave her a bemused look before shaking his head. "Do you always keep your phone there?"

She shrugged, blushing a little. "Only when necessary." Turning back to the kitchen, she called, "I'll be back before too terribly late!"

"Have a good time!" Linda called back.

Grace followed him out to his motorcycle,

frowning for a moment. How was she supposed to ride that thing in her skirt? She waited while he got on it, and then threw one leg over, keeping her skirts wrapped tightly around her legs. She put her arms around his waist and held on for dear life as he started the bike and roared out of the driveway.

He took them straight toward the mountains, and she was mesmerized by the way the sun was dancing down behind them. She looked at everything around her with wide eyes. The flowers were fully in bloom, and when they crossed a bridge over a river, she wondered if that was the same river Joy had once called her from.

It was so beautiful, but she wasn't sure if she was more fascinated by the beautiful scenery or the man she had her arms around so tightly.

Finally, after about thirty minutes, he pulled to the side of the road. "Look at that sunset," he said softly, pointing toward the mountains looming in front of them.

She took a picture of the sun as it was sinking below the mountains, taking a second to tweet it. *The sunset near my new home. Hello, Wyoming! #LazyLove*

After she'd typed in the hashtag, she frowned, but then shrugged. She was really only talking to fellow LLers anyway, so what did it matter?

Marcus watched her intently while she messed with her phone, his eyes memorizing her face. She was so beautiful. Living in a town filled with cowboys, she wasn't going to be single for long.

He cupped her face with one hand and lowered his lips to hers. "Hi."

She grinned. "Hi." She wasn't sure if she was happy or sad that he hadn't greeted her that way when he'd first arrived at the ranch. "How was your day?"

"Long. I thought of you a lot."

She blushed at that. "I thought of you too."

"What did you think of me?" he asked, curious. He'd had some pretty hot fantasies about her already, but he wouldn't be telling her that.

Grace blushed even redder. "I thought about how good it feels when you kiss me," she admitted.

"So you like kissing?"

"With you, I do."

He smiled at that. "Let's get back to my house then, and we can do lots more kissing."

"Sounds good to me. Besides, I'm hungry." She'd had time for a sandwich at lunch, but that had been many hours before.

"Ethel cooked. I don't know if she'll eat with us or not, but she's always welcome." That was non-negotiable for him. His housekeeper was more of another grandmother to him, and he wouldn't have any woman treating her rudely.

"That's fine. I'm not used to being alone with men anyway."

"I'm not just any man, though, right?" he asked, his eyes twinkling at her.

"You're not?"

He shook his head. "I'm the first man you've ever kissed. I guess you'll have to marry me."

Her heart jumped into her throat at his words. "I guess I will," she quipped back, trying to make light of it.

He turned around and drove them back to his house, parking his bike out front. He helped her off, and she handed him the helmet. She frowned when it was time to take it off. "I'm going to have hat hair!"

He laughed. "You'll be just as lovely in my eyes. I promise."

She sighed. It wouldn't do to tell him she wasn't usually vain, because as he got to know her, he'd realize that wasn't true. She always tried to look as ladylike as possible, but it just wasn't possible when you were taking a helmet off. "Maybe I'll just keep it on."

He reached out and unfastened her helmet for her, pulling it off her head. Her hair was flattened where the helmet had been, giving her a silly look. "You're still beautiful to me." He leaned down and brushed his lips across hers. "Let's eat."

Taking her hand, he led her into the house, calling out for Ethel as he walked in. "We're here!"

Ethel, a woman of indeterminate age and silver hair, popped her head around the corner. "Well, it's about time! You two take a detour to Cheyenne on the way? I expected you an hour ago!"

Marcus smiled at the older woman, used to her complaining. "Oh, Ethel, she hadn't seen the mountains yet! I had to take her to see the sunset!"

Ethel shook her head with a long-suffering sigh. "I suppose you did have to take her, but you should have called first. I know your mama taught you better manners than that!"

"Yes'm, she did. I'm so sorry. I'll remember next time!"

"You'd better!" She shook the spatula in her hand at him. "Go wash up. I'll put supper on the table."

Marcus pointed out a bathroom for Grace to use before taking the stairs two at a time. When he got back to the table, she was sitting quietly looking at her phone, her fingers flying. "Who're you talking to now?"

She grinned at him. "The star of my show, Valerie Savoy, saw my picture of the sunset on Twitter. She wants to know where I took it."

"Did you tell her that Culpepper is the most beautiful place on earth?" he asked.

She nodded. "I just did!"

"You're a smart woman."

Ethel brought the food in. "Now, I wasn't about to let my supper go to ruin by waiting for you two, not knowing when your shenanigans would bring you home, so I ate earlier. Put the dishes in the sink, and I'll wash them in the morning." She looked at Grace, wagging her finger in her face. "And if you think you're being a good person by washing them for me, you can think again, little missy! My kitchen, my dishes. You hear?"

Grace nodded. "Yes, ma'am." Her eyes were wide as she watched the woman walk back toward the kitchen. "Is she always like that?" She dropped her voice to a whisper, not wanting the old harridan to hear.

Marcus nodded. "Isn't she *awesome*?"

Grace giggled softly. "She is! I think I love her!"

"Don't let her hear you say that! She'll get even worse!"

"I won't." She took a bite of the chicken and dumplings the woman had prepared for them. "These are delicious."

Marcus nodded, sighing contentedly. "She's a wonderful cook. She has a hard time cleaning the upstairs because of her knees, but she does everything else to perfection. I'm so glad to have her here."

After they finished eating, Grace put the dishes into the sink, not daring to do anything more than rinse them off. Then she hurried into the living room to join Marcus on the couch. "What are we watching on?" she asked.

He nodded to the television mounted on the wall. "It's a smart TV. We can watch Netflix on it." He turned the object in question on with his remote, and quickly navigated the menu. "*Lazy Love*, right?"

"Yes. I sure hope you like it as much as I do."

He pulled up the first episode, wrapping his arms around her shoulders. "Just so we get to watch it together."

The first scene, one she'd watched just the night before for the umpteenth time, had her stomach filled with butterflies. She desperately wanted him to like her show. The scene showed Jo receiving a phone call in the middle of her English class at a prestigious all-women's college in the East. She left the room to take the call, and whatever she heard had her dropping her phone, and leaning back against the wall in defeat.

Then came the opening credits, and she smiled as she watched the different actors' faces flash on the screen. First Valerie Dobson as Jo Larson. Second was Jesse Savoy as Dr. Dylan Drake. And then Amber Knight as MaryBeth Larson. All the names were as familiar to Grace as those of her own sisters.

Marcus looked down at Grace, smiling at how excited she looked with the show on his television. So far, it looked boring to him, but he didn't care. It would give them something to do together, and during a movie was always a good time to kiss a girl.

The next scene showed Jo back in Texas on the ranch where she'd lived until her mother died when she was five. She'd then been shipped off to boarding school, only spending summers with her father and sister, who was five years younger. It came out as the story went on that her mother had died of an infection she'd gotten during childbirth.

MaryBeth was home from her own boarding school, and none too happy with living under her sister's roof.

Dr. Dylan Drake met both sisters at the funeral. He took Jo's hands into his. "I'm so sorry for your loss, Miss Larson."

"It's not a loss when you don't know the man being buried," she'd responded with her typical bluntness.

Dr. Drake had nodded. "I'm sorry for that loss as well then. I'm Dr. Dylan Drake, the local veterinarian."

"I'm sure I'll be seeing a lot of you then, Dr. Drake."

Bob, the ranch's foreman stood right behind Jo. "I'll alert you if you're needed, Dr. Drake. The family is thankful for your willingness to help." The man's eyes met Dylan's as he made it clear he had no intention of letting him swoop in and marry the beautiful woman in front of them.

"I'll be around regardless. No need for Miss Larson to have to learn about how to take care of all of the animals without help."

As Dylan walked out of the room, Marcus paused the show. "Okay, now which one is she married to in real life? It's one of those two, right?"

"Do you want me to tell you or do you want to figure it out on your own?"

"Well, I think it was the veterinarian guy. He's the one she seems to have some real chemistry with." He brought her fingers to his lips, thinking how much his chemistry with Grace reminded him of the chemistry onscreen.

"You're right. He's Jesse Savoy. The credits for the last three episodes have changed the heroine's name to Valerie Savoy."

"Wait, I might have read something about that one day. There was a headline about some actress dumping her boyfriend and marrying her co-star the same day. Valerie the Virgin? Am I right?"

"Yes! That's them. Valerie Dobson was called Valerie the Virgin before she married Jesse Savoy. And her ex-boyfriend has just been sentenced to thirty years in prison. I think it was a plea bargain or something. Rumor has it he kidnapped her sister, but I'm not sure if that's true."

Marcus frowned. "I think I read about that too. That's this show?"

She nodded emphatically. "And Valerie is the one who was messaging me on Twitter a little while ago!"

"She really tweets with fans?"

"Yes! That's part of what I find so incredible about the show. The fans and stars tweet live while the show is happening too. Jesse wasn't always involved in the Twitter parties before they married, but now he never misses an episode. And they usually take a selfie of the two of them sitting there with their phones tweeting away. They're always holding hands or she's in his lap or something." She sighed.

"What? You want to be in his lap?"

"Not at all. I just want someone to look at me the way Jesse looks at Valerie." She shrugged. "There's this great clip from them on the *Night Show*. It's so obvious that neither of them are acting, and their feelings are real! Matt Winters, the host, actually looks at Jesse and says, 'You get paid for that?' after this incredible kissing scene."

Marcus noted what she was saying. She wanted to be loved the way the stars of her show loved each other. He could start studying how they acted in their interviews and recreate it. He may be only a lawyer, but he could show this sweet girl the kind of romance she was craving. It wouldn't kill him.

By the time the show was over, she was yawning. "I'm sorry. We're working long days to get the bakery up and running as soon as possible."

He nodded. "I understand. I hate to add to your tiredness. Why don't I take you home?"

She frowned, turning her face into his shoulder. "I'm not ready to leave you yet."

Marcus smiled at that. "I appreciate the sentiment, but you need sleep. We can do this again tomorrow night."

She smiled at that. "Well, in that case…"

He put one finger under her chin and turned her face up to his for a kiss. "I need at least one good kiss before I can take you home, though."

Grace sighed. "I was afraid you were going to forget all about kissing me."

"How could I do that when it's all I've thought about all day?" Of course, he'd thought about doing a whole lot more than kissing her, but he wasn't going to discuss where his thoughts had really gone. She was too innocent to hear all that from him.

She lifted her lips for his kiss, one hand flattening against the front of his shirt, while the other went to the back of his neck to toy with the curls there. When his lips came down on hers, she felt her heart skip a beat. Oh, how he got her heart racing when he kissed her.

His arms closed around her, pulling her closer toward him. He wanted to pull her onto his lap, but he knew that would be a bit much. No, he'd have to content himself with holding her against him.

Her lips fluttered beneath his, responding to his. He traced the seam of her lips with his tongue, demanding entrance. "Open for me."

Grace got onto her knees on the couch beside him, pressing even closer. When he started to kiss her this way, she could think of nothing but getting closer to him and touching him. The hand at the front of his shirt, rubbed up and down his chest, feeling his hard muscles beneath the fabric of his shirt.

Finally, he pulled back, taking big gulps of air. "For someone who was never kissed before yesterday, you're awfully good at it."

She giggled. "Why, thank you." She'd never once in her life considered she would think that was a compliment, but here she was, loving every kiss. Was she more like Chastity than she'd realized?

"We have to get out of here. I'm too tempted to carry you up the stairs to my bed right now. That would not be a good idea at all."

She sighed. "Oh, I think it sounds like a fine idea, but I also think that I would hate myself forever if we did that before I had a ring on my finger."

He nodded, sighing. "And we're talking a wedding ring, not engagement ring, right?" He knew the answer, but he clarified anyway. He wanted to make sure they were on the same page about everything.

She nodded. "I was taught that an engagement ring means it's okay to hold hands. Not even time to kiss yet."

"All right. I may have to think about this a bit."

"Think about what?" She was still a bit too bemused from his kisses to be able to concentrate on what he was saying.

"About putting a wedding ring on that finger."

She stared at him, her eyes wide. "We've known each other for less than thirty-six hours."

Marcus shrugged. "How long do you think it took Jo and Dylan to know they belonged together?"

"I think he knew the instant their eyes met. She may have taken a little longer." Grace wasn't sure if he meant on the show or in real life, but with those two the answer seemed to be the same. Their chemistry together was too strong for it to be any other way.

He stood up. "Let's go. We'll take my truck this time. No reason for you to have to climb on my bike with your skirt again."

"Oh, it wasn't so bad. I'm used to doing everything I need to do in a skirt."

"Did you not wear pants at home?" he asked, leading her toward the front of the house where his truck was parked.

She shook her head. "Not very often. My parents thought girls should wear skirts at all times, because pants tempt men to do things they shouldn't. A girl should always be covered as much as possible."

"You know that's a bunch of hogwash, right?"

She laughed. "I always suspected it was. Thank you for confirming it for me."

He opened the truck door and waited as she got in before running around to the other side. "What time tomorrow night?" he asked. "I'm working from home tomorrow, so I'll be available after five or so."

She frowned, unsure how long the trip into town for supplies would take. "We're shopping tomorrow for supplies for the bakery. Why don't I text you when we're home, and I can get away? I can't leave my cousins to do all the work."

"Of course, you can't! I'd never ask you to!"

"Good. Give me your number, and I'll text as soon as I'm ready."

He rattled off his number as he pulled into Linda Culpepper's driveway. He parked the truck and unbuckled her seatbelt, pulling her across the seat to him. "One more kiss, and then I'll go on my merry way."

She offered her lips to him sweetly. "I'm already ready for the days when we won't have to kiss goodnight in your truck." She knew she was probably being too forward, at least her mother would have said so, but sometimes she needed to say what was on her mind.

He grinned at that. "Well, Miss Grace, hopefully those days will be over real soon."

Grace smiled as she opened the door, getting

down out of the truck. "You might need to install a step on my side. It's a big climb for a girl like me."

He laughed. "I'll do just that. G'night, Grace."

"G'night, Marcus." She turned and hurried into the house, looking back over her shoulder one last time before opening the door. He was pretty incredible in her eyes.

Chapter Five

Grace woke the next morning with a smile on her lips. She could still feel how good Marcus's lips felt against hers. She couldn't wait to spend more time with him, and they had agreed to get together that evening.

She groaned as she rolled out of bed, thinking about all the things she needed to get done before she would have that privilege. After a quick shower, she hurried into the kitchen to have breakfast. It was just her and Honor again, and she smiled at her twin. "Where is everyone?"

Honor shrugged. "Linda made breakfast, but said she had a couple of things to prepare for the kids today. The other two aren't up yet. Patience and Felicity aren't exactly morning people."

"They'll have to learn to be if they want to run a successful bakery!" Grace said, sipping her juice. "I had dinner with my Marcus last night."

"Your Marcus? I think I saw you two walking across the yard together on Sunday. It's hard to believe we've only been here two days." Honor shook her head. "So much has happened in such a short time!"

"What do you think of the horses?"

"Horses? Oh, they're awesome. I'm in love

already." Honor seemed a bit distracted to Grace. "How 'bout you? I heard you went on a walk with your lawyer man."

Grace grinned. "Well, I wouldn't say he's my lawyer-man. Yet."

"Tell me you didn't tell him any of your stupid lawyer jokes!"

Grace bit her lip to stifle a giggle. "One or two."

"Or fifty." Honor shook her head. "And they say you're the practical twin."

Grace shrugged. "Maybe I'm tired of being the practical twin. Time to live dangerously for a change."

Honor studied Grace over the top of her coffee cup. "Did he kiss you?"

Grace looked around. Linda had wandered off somewhere, and their cousins hadn't come to breakfast yet. "Yes."

"And? Did you like it?"

Grace sighed, knowing her eyes were sparkling. "Kissing is better than *Lazy Love*." She knew her twin would get the impact of her words.

Honor stared at her sister in disbelief for a moment, before throwing her head back and laughing. "You're a goner. Have you talked wedding yet?"

"No! We just met Sunday! He'd never seen *Lazy Love*, so I had to introduce him."

Honor rolled her eyes good-naturedly. "Of course you did. Because everyone on the planet needs to love that silly show just as much as you do."

Grace shrugged. "Well, it would be nice. It's the best show on television, after all."

"You just keep thinking that." Honor looked around to see who was there. "What else did you do? Did you have a good time?"

"We had a marvelous time. We walked across the ranch over to his house, which is on the other side of the woods. It's so beautiful here. I don't ever want to leave."

"Just don't tell Mom and Dad that when you call, and we'll be good. I don't want them to realize we're not coming back until we're at least seventy-three."

"Seventy-three? Why seventy-three?"

"Not sure." Honor shrugged. "Just seems like a good age, doesn't it?"

"Sure!" Grace reached out and squeezed her sister's hand. "I hope you have a great day today."

"Are y'all going to work on setting up the bakery?"

Grace nodded. "We have our first order. A baby shower cake."

"I hope word gets out fast. From what I hear, they need a lot of money."

"Who've you been talking to?"

"Angus. How did the lawyer like your silly show?"

"You can't call it silly unless you've seen it." Grace stuck her tongue out at her twin. She was still wearing her pajamas, and they looked very much alike in that moment. Neither had done the things that made them different. Honor wasn't wearing her "boy clothes" and Grace hadn't yet put on her make-up or fixed her hair. They deliberately emphasized their differences, and had for years, because they were sick of being seen as a matching set of salt and pepper shakers.

"Fine. Your potentially-silly show. Is that better?"

Grace wrinkled her nose. "I guess it's better. I think he liked it. Or else he's just tolerating it for me."

"Either way, he sounds like a good guy. I'm glad you like him."

"For someone I felt obligated to date at least once, he's pretty terrific. We're going to see each other again tonight. He's already mentioning rings."

"Oh, wow. Dad would have a fit!" Honor shook her head. "I wonder how they'll react when they realize we're all moving here."

Grace sighed. "I don't even want to think about it, to be honest with you. Dad will probably blame Mom for not taking us more in hand. Whatever." Grace hated the idea of making things harder on their mother, but she couldn't live under those conditions for another minute. She had the right to live her life as she saw fit, as long as she didn't break God's laws. And not the made-up laws that people attributed to God either.

"I guess it's not something we can worry about." She jumped up. "I need to get dressed, so I can go spend my day with the horses!" Honor shrugged, popping the last of her toast into her mouth in one huge bite. She was gone before Grace had a chance to ask any more questions.

Grace watched her go with a grin, wishing she could be more like Honor at times, but knowing it would only make Honor behave even more extreme so that they could still be as different as possible. She understood why Honor wanted to be an individual, but it still sometimes hurt that she didn't want to be anything like her.

They had to make a long drive into Cheyenne to go to a warehouse store, which would take a good half of the day. By the time they had everything put away and prepped for their first day open, there would be little time for anything else, before Marcus came to pick her up.

She finished her breakfast, put her plate in the dishwasher, and went to check on her cousins. If they were going to have a full day, they needed to start it early.

*****

Six hours later, Grace and her cousins were back from Cheyenne and unloading the SUV they'd borrowed from Hope. Grace was twitching slightly from all of the show tunes her cousins had sung on the trip. Didn't the girls know any songs other than show tunes? Grace was a fan, but not for hours straight. She wanted to kill someone!

Each of them had claimed a small workstation of their own for decorating. Grace set hers up with a smile, putting her tubes and food colorings in a logical order so she could get to them when she wanted.

She was still a bit mystified about how they'd advertise, but Linda kept assuring her that as long as she made cakes, people would buy them. "In a small town like Culpepper, you don't have to advertise," Linda assured her. "It's a lot harder to hide what you're doing than it is to broadcast it."

By the time they'd finished putting everything where they wanted it, and getting the bakery ready to start working in, it was after four-thirty. Grace hurried back to the big house and rushed through her shower. She couldn't see Marcus with the flour that had formed a light powder over her body as they had transferred it from the huge bags to the plastic bins they'd purchased to store it in.

She dressed in jeans instead of a dress, worried he might bring his motorcycle again, and she didn't want to feel uncomfortable with how she was dressed.

After she'd finished her show and was dressed and ready, she texted him. *Ready when you are. Did you have a good day?*

I don't know about good, but it was productive. Be there in ten minutes.

Grace wandered into the kitchen to talk to Linda. It was the first time she'd seen her all day. "I'm going to spend the evening with Marcus."

Linda smiled. "You and your sisters. You get out from under your parents' thumbs and go wild."

Grace frowned at that. "Does it seem like I'm going wild? We're not doing anything wrong. Just spending time together. He's never even touched me inappropriately!"

Linda shook her head. "Grace, it's okay! You're a big girl. I'm not your mother."

"But I don't want to do something that even gives the appearance of being wrong. Do you think I should take one of the other girls as a chaperone?"

"No, I don't. I think what you're doing is fine. I'm sorry if I made it seem like you were doing wrong, because I really don't think so." Linda hugged Grace. "Go and have a wonderful time."

Grace nodded, still unsure about how she should act with Marcus. Maybe she was being too forward by going to his house with him every night. Maybe she should tell him that she couldn't spend any more time alone with him until they were married. She knew most people didn't feel those things were necessary, but she had been raised to believe they were.

The knock came at the door then, and Grace hurried toward it. "I won't be too late!" she called back to Linda.

"Just enjoy yourself!"

Grace opened the door and smiled. Marcus stood there, leaning against the door jam, looking sexier than any man had a right to look. The look in his eyes made her feel weak in the knees. "Hi you."

The grin that spread across his face did nothing for the state of her knees. "Hi." He took her hand, leading her out to his truck. "Did you get a lot done today?"

She nodded, running her hand over the back of her neck, surprised at the tension she felt as a result of one teasing comment. "We did. The bakery is all ready to start tomorrow."

"Wow. You girls are sure moving fast." He didn't bother to start the truck and instead pulled her toward him. "I missed your kisses today."

She wrapped her arms around his neck, drawing his head down for a kiss. "I missed yours too." How could a man's kisses be so addictive? He always had a very distinct taste to him. Kind of orangey. How did he do that?

After a moment, he pulled back and started the truck, driving out onto the highway. "If we're going to keep doing this, we need to build a road between the Culpepper's house and mine. It would take less than half the time if I could just drive straight and not go in a big U."

She shrugged. "Probably." Her mind was back on what Linda had said. He expected her to kiss him as soon as they were alone. How long would that last before he'd expect more? No wonder her mother had said to save kissing for marriage.

"You all right?" he asked, surprised that she seemed so moody. She was normally very even tempered. He thought about asking if it was that time of the month, but thought better of it. A girl had threatened him with a steak knife for that once.

She nodded. "Just thinking."

"Want to talk about it?" Whatever it was, he wanted things out in the open with her.

"You know how I was raised. We've talked about it." At his nod, she continued. "Linda made an innocent comment a few minutes ago about how when my sisters and I get away from our parents, we go nuts. I—it's got me thinking maybe us spending so much time together isn't a good idea."

Marcus frowned. "Is that how you really feel? Or is that how your parents would feel?"

"Well, it's definitely how my parents would feel. I guess I've always kind of believed it too. More than any of my sisters did anyway. I didn't drink *all* the Kool-Aid. Only half a jug! I like spending time with you, and I don't think kissing before marriage is wrong, but we sure are putting ourselves into a situation where temptation could be very easy."

He pulled into his driveway, before turning to her. "Ethel is out for the evening. It's just going to be us. If you don't want to be totally alone, I can take you into town for dinner. There's not much there, but I'd be happy to go."

"I know you think I'm being silly, and I probably am, but—old habits die hard."

"I know they do." He took her hand, enfolded it in his big one. "I wasn't raised like you are. My grandfather is a minister, and he sure preaches sex before marriage is wrong, but he sees nothing wrong with kissing before marriage. I honestly didn't know anyone thought that was wrong until a few years ago."

"That's because you've never met my parents." She sighed. "I don't want to disappoint you, but I don't want to disappoint them either."

"So if we decided to get married on Saturday, would you feel right about spending this evening alone with me?"

She shrugged. "I don't know. I guess I'd be a little less worried. Not as much time for things to explode in our faces."

"I bought you a ring today," he said. He hadn't planned on blurting it out, but he wanted to get it out in the open. "I was planning to ask you while we were eating dinner."

"I'm not even sure how to react to that." She stared at him, her eyes wide. "You really went out and bought me a ring today?"

He nodded. "I did. I was planning to ask you, but I was going to wait for a few hours. I can still ask you at dinner if you want. I can make it nice and pretty for you."

She shook her head. "I don't need a big formal proposal. I guess I'd prefer you not get down on one knee and say, 'Let's get hitched,' but just a simple proposal is fine."

"But you want me to propose?" he asked.

She nodded. "Yeah, that'd be really nice."

He grinned. "Then I'll do it over dinner as I planned. Pretend to be surprised, would you? I thought about this a lot."

"I'll do my best."

They got out of the truck and went inside. Ethel had left chicken spaghetti and garlic bread warming in the oven. There was a salad waiting on the counter. Grace shooed Marcus from the kitchen while she served it. When she walked into the dining room to join him, he had the lights dimmed and two candles lit the small room.

She smiled at him. He really had planned to

make it a romantic meal. She set both plates on the table before taking her seat. "This looks delicious."

He nodded. "You're going to be all right with Ethel staying on after we marry, right? You won't feel the need to take over all the cooking?" He worried about the old woman who was so close to his grandmother. He didn't know where she'd go if she didn't get to stay there.

"Of course! It's not my purpose in life to completely change yours." She took a bite of the spaghetti. "And she's a very good cook!"

He grinned. "I think so too."

She had just pushed her plate away, when he took her hand. "Grace."

She looked back at him, knowing this was probably the moment he'd been working at building toward. "Yes?"

"Will you do me the honor of sharing your life with me?"

She smiled at the way he'd worded his question. He wasn't just asking her to marry him, he wanted her to share his life. "Yes, I would be thrilled."

He pressed a kiss to her hand before sliding a ring onto her finger. "I hope I got the right size. I had Joy ask Honor."

She nodded, staring down at the ring with the tiny diamond. Her eyes lit up. "It's beautiful."

"You really like it? I just thought that one suited you best."

"I love it. You did good."

"I considered asking Joy to go with me, but I

didn't want a Culpepper fist through my face."

Grace grinned. "You and Kolby don't get along?"

He shrugged. "Honestly, I don't have a problem with any of them. Chris was something of a rival in high school, but that's water under the bridge at this point."

She leaned toward him, brushing her lips lightly across his. "Do you really want to marry on Saturday?" she asked.

"Oh, if it were up to me, we'd get married tonight. I guess I can wait until Saturday."

She laughed. "I'd like to have time to bake us a wedding cake at least."

"I never thought of that. It makes sense that would be important to you." He stood from the table and led her to the living room by her hand. "Want to sit on the couch and smooch while we watch your show?"

"Sounds divine. I need to get the dishes in the sink first, though. They'll drive me crazy otherwise."

"Oh, you're one of those! Maybe I should have known that about you before I asked you to marry me."

She glared at him. "I have no idea what you're talking about, but I'm sure I don't care. I'm me."

He laughed. "I'll set the show up, while you get the dishes in the sink."

Ten minutes later, she joined him on the couch, curling up close to his side. "I like spending time with you."

"Because I watch your show with you?" he asked, his thumb hovering over the play button.

"Well, I do like that, I have to say. None of my sisters would ever watch it with me." She shook her head. "No, I enjoy spending time with you because I like you. A lot. Are we crazy to get married when there's only a lot of like going on?"

He shook his head. "I don't think so. So many marriages fail when people think they're madly in love. It burns out."

"Do you know a lot of people who have divorced?" Grace didn't know anyone who had ever divorced. People she knew stuck it out no matter what.

He nodded. "Unfortunately. I do a lot of family law. I hate watching couples fall apart and then fight over their children. No one ever wins."

"I'm sorry you have to do that. I wish everyone just stayed together forever."

"Me too." He pushed the play button, snuggling her close to his side. He didn't mind her show, because he rarely actually looked at the people on it. No, he spent his time looking at her instead. He loved watching her face change with the scenes.

They made it through two episodes that night before she had to go. "Tomorrow is going to be interesting. We're all going to bake like crazy to get an inventory, before we actually open our doors to the public on Thursday."

"So you can't sit on my couch and kiss me all

night long?"

She shook her head. "Only in my dreams."

"Well, if you promise to dream about kissing me…"

She pulled his head down for a quick kiss. "There. Will that sustain you for an hour or two?"

He shrugged. "I wouldn't object to another six or seven kisses…"

"You're getting greedy!"

"Wait 'til we're married. You don't know greedy yet!"

She blushed, trying not to let his words bother her. "Well, it'll all be right then."

"I understand." Dropping one more kiss onto her lips, he got to his feet and led her to the door.

"I almost forgot…"

"What?"

"What do you get when you cross a blonde and a lawyer?"

"Careful now. You're a blonde."

"I don't know. There are some things even a blonde won't do."

He grabbed her in a bear hug, kissing her neck. "No more lawyer jokes!"

"No more tonight. I agree."

"Is ever too much to ask for?"

"Oh, most definitely!" She winked at him. "You know how much I love lawyer jokes. I don't know what you'd do without them."

"I think I could make it through. In fact, I'm sure of it."

Once they were in the truck, she looked down

at her hand. "I love my ring."

"Good. I can't wait 'til Saturday."

"Any idea what time?" she asked.

"What time does the bakery close?"

"I think we decided four."

"How about seven then? Do you mind if my grandfather marries us?"

"Not if it's legal. I'd rather be able to tell my parents we were married by a minister anyway."

Marcus drove the short distance to the Culpepper ranch. "Do you have a car?" he asked. He couldn't believe he hadn't thought of that. He could take her back and forth, of course, but it would be easier if she had her own.

She shook her head. "I need to leave the car Honor and I share for her. And I can't afford to buy one until the Culpeppers have paid off Travis."

He knew she'd come to help out, so he asked nothing beyond that. "We'll make it work." His mind was racing. He wasn't rich, but he certainly had enough money saved up to buy her a truck. He would rather she had a four-wheel drive in Wyoming in the winter anyway. They had several months before they needed to worry about that, though. For now, something to drive her back and forth was all she needed.

He stopped in front of Linda's house, cutting the engine. "A kiss good night?" he asked.

"How did you ever survive without my kisses?"

"I have no idea..."

After a moment, he sighed. "I'm going to

have to let you out. Tomorrow night?" He stroked her arm, not wanting their time together to end so soon.

She thought about it for a moment. She had so much to do, but she really didn't want to avoid seeing him. "That would be good. Do you have a minute now?"

He nodded. "Why?"

"You haven't met my twin yet. I want you to." She hoped Honor was home. She really felt like she was doing something wrong by getting engaged to a man her twin hadn't met yet.

"Are you two close?"

"As close as identical twins who are nothing alike can be."

Marcus thought about that as he got out of the truck and walked around, taking her hand in his. "Why are you nothing alike?"

She shrugged. "More than anything I think it stemmed from the fact that our mother loved the whole identical thing. She always dressed us alike. She put the same bows in our hair." Grace shook her head. "So Honor went one way, and I went the other."

"Meaning?" He imagined Honor running around in a clown's suit, hoping that wasn't the case.

"Well, I'm super self-conscious about how I dress. I'm always in neat, tidy clothes. Honor dresses like a man. She refuses to wear dresses, no matter how mad it makes our parents. She likes everything outdoorsy. She's really getting dressed up if she puts her hair into a ponytail. For me, a ponytail is sloppy. You'll never have trouble telling us apart."

"It doesn't sound like I will." He shook his head. "So I need to expect you but not you."

She grinned. "Kind of, but not really." She opened the front door, her eyes searching for a sign of life.

To her delight, Honor was in the living room with Linda. When her sister looked up at her, she grinned. "So this must be Marcus, the great white shark...I mean, lawyer."

"Same thing!" Grace said quickly, giggling.

Honor winked at her sister, getting to her feet and going over to meet Marcus. "Sorry. I couldn't resist channeling Grace for just one second."

Marcus looked at the girl in front of him. Her face was very like Grace's, but she wore no make-up at all. She wore jeans and a button-up shirt, which was the same as what Grace was wearing, but she wore it so differently. Her shirt was untucked, and there was mud on her jeans. She smelled like she'd just come in from the stable. "Hi, Honor. I'm glad to meet you."

Honor nodded. "It's nice to meet you, too."

Grace held her hand out for Honor to see the ring. "We're getting married Saturday."

Honor smiled, hugging Grace. "Congratulations."

"You'll be my maid of *honor*, right?"

Honor laughed at the pun. "Only if I get to wear pants."

"As far as I'm concerned, you can show up in what you're wearing. It won't hurt me any."

"I might just do that. You never can tell."

Chapter Six

The first day of actual baking in the new facility told Grace and her cousins that they needed to rearrange again. They spent more than an hour on it before they were all satisfied. They had put all of the pre-made treats into a bakery display case they'd rented.

"It looks good," Grace said, admiring their handiwork.

"I just hope people buy stuff!" Patience said with a frown. She was in charge of running the cash register, at least at first. She'd made a huge variety of pies, and they were waiting to be purchased.

"I'm going to make some fresh bread in the morning as well," Grace said. "Nothing smells as good as fresh bread baking." She looked at her phone. It was later than she'd expected to finish.

She quickly texted Marcus. *It's after seven. I don't think I have time to come over and still be at work in the morning. Can you come here for a quick visit? Or we might have to skip tonight.*

The response was immediate. *I'll come over there. I want to at least see you.*

Give me an hour.

She didn't want him to see her with frosting on her pants. She'd worn an apron, but sometimes messes still happened.

She hurried back, showered, and was ready for him when he arrived. She led him to the living room, which was empty except for the two of them. "I'm glad you decided to come."

"I couldn't stay away. You only kiss me enough to fuel me for one day."

"So if I give you double kisses tonight?"

"I'll need quadruple tomorrow night. You probably shouldn't feed the beast."

"And you're the beast? Does that make me Belle?"

"You're the belle of my ball!" Marcus laughed and shook his head. "You're making me corny."

She grinned. "I think you were already there!" She looked at him. "I got a really strange and exciting tweet today."

"Oh? What was that?"

"The stars from *Lazy Love* are going to be in Culpepper this weekend. They invited me to have coffee with them on Sunday." She had been tweeting with them for so long, she felt like they were close friends.

He blinked a couple of times. "What did you say?"

"I didn't know what to say, so I thought I'd talk to you about it first. I could invite them to dinner, but would that be weird?"

"It wouldn't be weird if it wasn't the day after we got married and the only day we'll be able to take totally alone."

"I'll tell them I can't meet them." She was a bit disappointed, because she'd wanted to meet Valerie and Jesse for years, but the man beside her was more important than a couple of celebrities.

"No, don't do that. Tell them you're getting married Saturday, but you and your husband will meet them at the café in town for coffee on Sunday afternoon."

"You really don't mind?"

He shook his head. "I know how important this is for you. I don't mind at all." He would have preferred spending the day alone with her, of course, but how could he refuse to let her do something that would mean so much to her?

"Thank you!" She reached over and pulled his head down to hers for a kiss. "I'll tweet her tomorrow."

"What are they doing in Culpepper?"

She shrugged. "I have no idea. She asked about the sunset picture I posted. Maybe they want to be able to see it for themselves. That's the only thing I can think of."

"Maybe. I guess we'll find out on Sunday."

She changed the subject then, talking about the changes they'd had to make in the bakery after working there for a day. "We thought we had it just right, but we moved everything around after we stopped baking for the day. That's why we didn't finish until late."

"I remember what it's like to set up a new office."

"How was your day?" she asked. Her mother

had always drilled into them that no matter what a man did, it was more important than what his wife did, so he should get to talk about his day first.

"Oh, it was fine. Busy. I'm dealing with a messy divorce and custody battle. One of the underwear models is leaving his wife."

"That's sad. And they have a kid?"

He nodded. "A little two-year-old girl named Anna. Sweet as can be."

"Where do you think she'll end up?"

He shrugged. "I have no idea. I'm representing the mother, and I do hope it's her. The father travels too much."

"I really hope we don't end that way," she said.

He shrugged. "How could we? We're not going to give up and get a divorce. I don't think that option is in either of our minds. I think the majority of people who divorce are people who went into marriage thinking that they could easily end it if things didn't work out. If you're not going in with forever on your mind, then what's the point of even marrying?"

"I have no idea." She yawned widely. "Can I get you a snack? Something to drink?"

He shook his head and got to his feet. "No. You can walk me to the door, though. I know tomorrow is a really big day for you, and I don't want to make it hard on you."

She smiled, taking the hand he offered. "I'm sorry I'm so sleepy. I feel like you should come first, but I came here to do a job, and I need to do it."

"You're not doing anything wrong." When they got to the door, he cupped her face in both hands and kissed her. "I'm sorry we didn't have time to watch the show tonight."

She shrugged. "I don't have to watch it every day!" She would, though. After he left, she'd find one of her favorite episodes, but she would only watch the scenes where Jo and Dylan appeared together. What else about the show was even worth watching?

He pulled her to him, kissing her passionately. "I'm ready to call you wife."

She nodded, blushing a little. She wanted to be his wife and spend forever with him, but she didn't want to make love. It sounded awfully messy to her.

"Are you having second thoughts?" he asked.

She shook her head emphatically. "No, I want to marry you."

"Then what do I see in your eyes?"

"Nothing. I'm good."

He frowned, but didn't want to keep her there any longer. "We'll talk about it tomorrow night."

She just smiled at him. "Thanks for coming over."

"No problem."

*****

He was the first customer the following morning. "Got any muffins?" he asked her cousin, Patience, who was working the counter.

Grace heard him from her workstation. "I'll take care of this one, Patience." She grinned at

Marcus. "But first, meet my fiancé, Marcus."

Patience smiled at Marcus. Patience and Felicity had been raised very similarly to the Quinlan sisters, but the main difference was, they'd been homeschooled in an isolated atmosphere. Patience was a bit of a mouse when it came to men. She didn't know how to talk to them, and really had no desire to. Grace firmly believed that someone could be homeschooled and not turn out socially awkward, but her aunt had not been able to accomplish that.

After Patience walked away, Grace took Marcus's hand, squeezing it. "I feel like I should kiss you good morning, but there's this big counter between us. And I don't know how I feel about kissing in public."

"If you're only kissing me because you feel like you should, then you need to keep your kisses to yourself."

Grace frowned. "I didn't mean it that way."

"What time do you want me to come by later?" he asked, looking at the three different kinds of muffins in the display case.

The baked goods that weren't a specialty of any of the three bakers were made by rotation. It had been Felicity's day with the muffins.

"We're closing at four every day. If you come around five, that'll give me time to change and shower."

He frowned at that. "Do you shower before I pick you up every evening?"

She nodded. "Of course I do. Otherwise I'm

going to be covered in flour or sugar or frosting. I'm going to always look my best for you."

"You are?"

"Yes. Not obsessively." Probably not obsessively. When she'd been a teenager, she'd always imagined she would sneak out of bed and fix her hair and do her make-up before her husband could wake up and catch her with a clean face. She'd outgrown those ideas at least.

"I hope not obsessively. It won't matter to me if you're in make-up with your hair all fixed or wearing your hair in a ponytail."

"Maybe you should be marrying Honor..."

"No way. That's not the Quinlan twin I'm attracted to."

She grinned, putting one of each flavor muffin in a bag for him. "These are on me. I gave you an orange, a blueberry, and a mixed berry."

"Oh, yum. They sound good."

She hurried to the side counter and poured some coffee into a to-go cup for him. "I hope you enjoy."

"Oh, I will." He winked at her. "See you at five."

"I'll text if it'll be any later than that."

*****

She texted at four. *I didn't think about clean up time. I can't leave that for my cousins. Can we make it six?*

As always, he responded immediately. *Six is fine. Dinner at my place?*

Yes, please.

*****

When he got there at six, she was still blow drying her hair. Patience brought him to her door. "She's getting ready."

Marcus opened the door and sat on her bed while Grace finished up. Patience had called to her that he was there, but she obviously didn't hear, because she came out of her bathroom in jeans and a lacy bra. "Nice."

Grace blushed, grabbing the blouse she'd planned to wear and holding it in front of her. "Where did you come from?"

"Patience told you I was here, but I guess you didn't hear her." He was amused by how mortified she looked.

"Obviously." She hurried into the bathroom and shut the door behind her, shrugging the shirt on and buttoning it before going back into her bedroom. "I'm sorry you had to see me that way."

"Had to?" he asked. "I assure you, it was my pleasure."

She frowned at that. "My mom says that men should never see women partially clothed before they're married because it will send them into a frenzy of lust, and it would be the girl's fault."

Marcus grinned. "Well, I don't know about a frenzy of lust, but I think you looked beautiful."

She couldn't meet his eyes. "I really am sorry."

He could see she was mortified. He'd been treating the whole thing as a joke, but it meant a great deal to her. "Hey. It's all right. I'm not upset at all."

"I really didn't mean to tempt you that way before we ever got married. I know it's not right."

He shook his head. "I know it was an accident. But even if it hadn't been, there are girls a lot more scantily clad on every beach in America. If I can't control my hormones, that's my problem, not yours."

"I—I know better, and I never should have done that."

He grabbed her hand and pulled her to stand between his spread legs as he sat on the bed. "Grace, look at me. You didn't know I was here. You'd never have come out with no shirt on if you had. We're going to be married in two days. The world isn't going to end because I saw you without a shirt on."

She took a deep breath, her eyes meeting his. "Thank you for not being angry with me."

"I'll never be angry over an accident."

"You're a good man," she said softly, thinking about the many times her father had yelled at her mother for things that were out of her mom's control.

"I hope you knew that before you agreed to marry me," he said with a wink.

"I had my suspicions."

He pulled her down onto his lap, holding her close. When she sat stiffly in his arms, he frowned at her. "What's wrong, Grace?"

She sighed. "I'm just a little nervous about everything. We're getting married so quickly, and I want to be your wife, I do. I just don't know if—well, if I'm ready for the sexual part of marriage."

"Why wouldn't you be?" he asked softly. "You like it when I kiss you, don't you?"

She nodded. "To be really frank, I don't know a lot about it. Only what my mom told me."

He was almost afraid to ask. "What exactly did your mom tell you?"

"She said I had to let my husband touch me however he wants, but that I wouldn't like it much, so I should just close my eyes and plan out my meals for the week. She said if a woman is lucky, her husband will be satisfied with once per week." She shrugged. "But I won't be able to plan out meals, because Ethel takes care of all that, so I'm not sure what to do!"

Marcus closed his eyes for a moment, trying to contain his anger at the woman he'd never met. "Well, what do you think about that? When I kiss you, does it feel good to you?" He watched her closely as he asked the question, needing to understand how she really felt.

She blushed, nodding. "Yeah, you know it does."

"Does it only feel good where our lips are touching? Or in other places too?"

Grace refused to look at him, but shook her head. "Other places."

"I think we're going to be fine, Grace. But, just to be clear. I'm going to want it more than once per week."

Her eyes widened as she peeked at his face,

trying to determine if he was joking with her again. "Really?"

Marcus nodded emphatically. "Really."

She took a breath. "Maybe I should talk to one of my older sisters about it."

"I'm fine with that. It's your decision. If it's not too embarrassing to talk to one of them, then do that. If it is, we'll handle it on our own."

"I'll try. Joy and I have always been really close. I'm sure she'll talk to me if I need her to."

He nodded, pulling her head down for a quick kiss. "If you can't get the answers you need from her, please talk to me about it instead of just worrying. Was that what was bugging you last night too?"

"Yeah. It just sounds so messy."

He grinned. "A little bit. But it's so worth it!"

"What about kids. Do you want kids right off?"

He carefully pushed her to her feet before standing. "Let's talk about this while we drive. You still okay with going to my house tonight?"

She nodded. "Yeah." She grabbed her phone. "Oh, coffee at two at the café with Valerie and Jesse. I'm really excited to meet them. I've been tweeting with them for four years now. Thank you for agreeing to do that."

"That'll be fun for you then."

"And for you?"

"Watching how happy it makes you will be reward enough for me." He took her hand and pulled her toward the front door.

In the truck, he glanced at her. "How do you feel about kids right off? 'Cuz I could really go either way. I want kids eventually, but you're young. If you want to wait a year or five to start having children, I'm all for it."

She bit her lip. "So we'd just abstain?"

He shook his head adamantly, glad he hadn't started driving yet when she asked that. Why, he may have driven right off the road. "No, we use birth control."

"Birth control? But that's against God!"

He took her hand in his. "Your mom told you that?"

She nodded. "You should only have sexual relations within marriage, and then only with the intentions of procreation."

He blinked. "You know you don't have a baby every time you have sex, right?"

She shrugged. "Well, I know you sometimes have to try more than once for a baby. But then you stop once you're pregnant, right?"

"No, you don't. Women make love all through their pregnancy."

"So how do we prevent it if we don't want children?"

"Did you not have sex ed in school?" He had a hard time believing that a woman her age could be so sexually naïve in this day and time. "We'll either use condoms or you can get on the birth control pill. There are also shots, I think."

"Our doctor back home said that only women who wanted to ruin themselves forever used birth control."

"Don't tell me. He was a friend of your parents?"

She nodded. "He played golf with Daddy every Wednesday. How'd you know?"

"Just a lucky guess, I suppose." He sighed heavily. "You know that he lied to you, right? Birth control is perfectly safe. If you're afraid of it, we can use condoms, though." He'd never had sex without a condom, so it didn't really matter that much to him.

"Do you know of a doctor who would prescribe birth control?"

He nodded. "There's actually a doctor in town who is a female. Her name is Dr. Ross. She's really sweet. Her younger sister is a midwife, and they share a house."

"So she's single?"

"Yeah."

"Why didn't you date her?"

"Do you really wanna know?" He pulled into his driveway and unbuckled his seat belt.

She nodded. "Yeah."

"Well, she was a couple years ahead of me in school, and she was so smart, she made me uncomfortable. So I never asked her out."

"What about her sister?" It seemed strange a lawyer would be intimidated by an intelligent woman.

"I don't know. I think because her sister intimidated me." He hadn't really ever thought about either of them as potential girlfriend material.

"I see." She scooted closer to him, touching his arm. "I don't intimidate you, do I?"

He shook his head, leaning down to give her a playful kiss. "No, you make me hot! Big difference."

She blushed at his words. "You're really not supposed to say that to me!"

Marcus frowned. "Well, you don't want me saying it to other women do you? If not you, then who?"

She refused to answer that, moving across the seat to open her door. "You're out of control sometimes, you know."

"Do you want me to make you an appointment with Dr. Ross?" he asked, before she could get out of the truck. He liked the idea of her being on birth control. Waiting a year or two for children, with as young as she was, seemed like the best idea all around.

She nodded. It made her nervous, but she'd do it. She wasn't ready for babies right away anyway.

Chapter Seven

By Saturday morning, Grace was certain the bakery would be a success. She was glad she'd started making the bread and cinnamon rolls every morning, because they disappeared quickly along with the muffins. She stood at her workstation, carefully putting the finishing touches on the baby shower cake that would be picked up in less than an hour.

She still had a bit to do with the wedding cake she was making for her and Marcus, but that wouldn't be a problem.

"I'm surprised how many people come here to buy their breakfast," Grace told Felicity, who was working at her own station, decorating some specialty cookies for a birthday party.

"I know. I thought people went to the café for everything." Felicity squirted some white icing in an arc, creating Elsa's hair for the *Frozen* themed party.

Patience took care of three customers, before sitting down for a moment. "My pies don't sell as well as the cookies, cakes, and muffins. Maybe I should learn to make something else."

"I think your pies will be a lot more popular around Thanksgiving and Christmas," Grace told her cousin. "Maybe you could learn to make scones?"

"Oh, that sounds like a fun challenge." Patience pulled out her phone to search for a recipe. "These look good!" The excitement that went through her at the idea of learning something new was palpable.

"Remember, I'm taking off at three today. I need to get ready to get married."

"We know. I can't believe Honor is going to be your maid of honor in a pair of pants. You'd think she could dress appropriately for her own twin's wedding," Felicity said, while wrinkling her nose.

"She's wearing dress pants. Dressing in pants is just what Honor does. You guys never had to deal with losing who you were by being part of a set of multiples. With Honor and I looking the same, we had to do something to distinguish ourselves."

"I still think she should dress correctly."

Grace took a deep breath. "And I think you should mind your own business. Honor can wear anything she wants to my wedding. She's my twin, and I love her."

Felicity looked shocked at Grace's words. "I'd think *you* would care."

"Well, I don't. I'm just glad she's willing to stand up with me." Grace looked up at the bell on the door. It was Marcus, and she grinned when she saw him. "Hi you!"

He walked around the counter and grabbed her, kissing her. "Sorry, I just had to do that." He winked at Patience, who refused to look at him. "Do you have any muffins left?'

"We made a double batch this morning, because we expected extra people on Saturday. Turns out it was a smart move. Only three left!" Grace said, grinning at him. "Is your grandpa ready to marry us?"

"As ready as he ever is," Marcus said with a grin. "Hopefully he'll remember your name."

Grace shrugged. "I don't know. I loved the way he addressed Hope during her wedding. At least what I've heard of it." She was still sad she'd missed out on her four older sisters' weddings.

"He didn't call her 'insert bride's name here' did he? I've seen him do that before, and it's so embarrassing."

Grace laughed, the sound of it filling the bakery. "He did! I didn't know he'd done that with anyone else."

"Oh, he does it all the time. He never remembers the names of any of the brides. I keep telling him to just write them on his hand, but he says he'd forget which hand. I suggest both, and he complains he can only write on his left, because he's right handed. Well, then why wouldn't he remember he'd written it on his left hand?" Marcus shook his head with a sigh. "It's going to be an interesting wedding."

"At least when we're done we'll be officially married." She smiled at him tentatively.

He grinned. "We will. I'm counting down the hours."

*****

The ceremony was beautiful, even though Brother Anthony did forget Grace's name. Instead, he called her "pretty blond girl." She accepted it with a smile.

At the end of the ceremony, he pronounced them licensed to kiss. Marcus took her into his arms and kissed her passionately. "I like being licensed to kiss."

"Yes, but as your wife, you still have to get *my* permission to kiss me." She said, smiling up at him teasingly.

"Oh, sure. I'll ask permission every time. I won't just grab you and start kissing you whenever I feel like it. Never." He lowered his head to kiss her right then, proving himself a liar.

Linda came over to hug Grace. "Are you coming back to the house tonight? I didn't get a chance to really plan a wedding reception."

Grace smiled. "We're using the church's fellowship hall, and the cake I made is in there already. All we're serving is cake and punch. Miss Lovie made the punch."

Linda nodded. "I'd have been happy to help."

"You're busy enough with the daycare and all the extra guests you keep ending up with. Don't you think?"

"Do you want me to agree with you? Or do you want me to tell you the truth?" Linda asked.

"Oh, agree with me this time, would you? You can tell me the truth next time." Grace turned to Honor, hugging her tightly. "I love that outfit," she said with a smile. "You look beautiful."

"Oh, anything but beautiful!" Honor protested, a grin on her face. "You made a stunning bride, Grace."

Marcus took Grace's hand and led her into the fellowship hall, where she met a few people from the church. "Oh, and this is Dr. Ross," he told her. "You have an appointment with her on Monday afternoon."

Grace nodded. "All right. I can do that."

"I'll give you directions sometime before then."

One of Grace's favorite things about the reception was to be able to watch Marcus's housekeeper, Ethel, with his grandmother. They were obviously very close.

Marcus followed her gaze and whispered to her, "Ethel is going to spend a week with my grandmother. She'll come over while you're working to clean and fix meals, but she doesn't think anyone should stay in the house with us while we're still newlyweds."

Grace nodded. "That makes sense to me." She knew she'd be a lot less embarrassed about the things they'd be doing if there was no one else in the house with them.

"Let's cut the cake and get out of here. She said she left dinner in the oven."

She nodded, her hand shaking. She was more nervous than she thought she'd be. "We'll have to coordinate getting my stuff from the back of Honor's car."

He nodded to let her know he'd heard her as

they cut the cake together. "Sounds good. Should only take a minute."

"Yeah, I don't think it's a big deal, I just wanted you to know that we needed to do it. I need clothes for the weekend."

"Don't fuss on my account," he said, a wicked smile on his face.

She contemplated smooshing the wedding cake on his face, just to get rid of that smile, but she'd always thought it was rude and a waste of her delicious cake. Instead, she fed him a small bite with her fingers, feeling him lick the cake off her thumb.

The touch of his tongue on her skin had a shiver running through her. "Stop!" she said, blushing.

He lowered his head, so his lips were against her ear. "I can't. You like it too much."

"I do? Are you sure?"

He nodded. "I'll show you later."

She didn't answer, turning away to talk to her sister, Chastity, who pressed a gift into her hands. "Do you want me to open it now?"

Chastity shook her head. "I think you'll be much happier with yourself if you wait and open it later."

"Then that's what I'll do," Grace said, trying to keep the relief from her voice. She could only imagine what Chastity thought was an appropriate wedding gift.

Fifteen minutes later, they were transferring her things from the back of Honor's car to the backseat of Marcus's truck. "There. Ready?"

Grace hugged Honor one last time. "It's going to seem weird not living under the same roof. I know we've barely seen each other in the past week, but I knew I could go to your room and talk to you whenever I wanted."

"Well, I'm getting married on Tuesday anyway, so we still wouldn't have lived together."

"Wait. What? You're getting married Tuesday?"

"Angus. I'll introduce you. He came with me."

"Wait, was he the guy running around in a kilt and looking at you like he wanted to eat you for lunch?"

Honor shrugged. "Might have been."

"There was only one man in a kilt. That was him?"

"Yeah, that was him."

"I want to meet him very soon!"

"If we get a chance to go by the bakery, you can." Honor raised a hand in farewell before slipping behind the wheel of the car and driving off.

"I worry about her sometimes," Grace said to Marcus.

"Why?"

"Because she's so determined to be different from me, that I think she's almost afraid to be herself."

Marcus nodded. "I can understand that."

Grace walked around to the other side of his truck and climbed in, tucking her long dress around her legs. She was ready to get back to his place. It had been a long day, and she was getting tired. She may not know much about sex, but even she knew he'd be offended if she fell asleep while they were making love.

Marcus drove them toward the ranch. "You look so tired. What time have you been getting up?"

"I try to be at the bakery by five each morning, so I've been waking up about four to get ready. I just grab food there."

He frowned. "And I've been keeping you out until at least nine. We're going to have to start going to bed earlier. You need more sleep than that."

"Or I can catch a quick nap when I get home every day. That would work too."

"I guess it would." He frowned over at her. "Are you excited to meet Valerie and Jesse tomorrow?" They'd watched the first half of the first season of her show, and he'd finally seen the couple kiss for the first time. He didn't get the appeal until he saw the raw chemistry between them as soon as they'd touched. He was interested to see if it would be the same in real life.

"There's dinner in the oven for us," he said, before carrying her suitcases upstairs to his room.

She was clutching the gift Chastity had given her, and she opened it while he was out of the room. It was a teal nightgown with lace that came to mid-calf. It was beautiful and matched her eyes perfectly. Only that morning had she realized she had no sexy lingerie to wear for her wedding night, so she was thrilled with the gift. She was surprised at her sister's taste, having expected something trashier.

She carefully stuffed it back into the box while she plated a couple of meals for her and Marcus. She was just setting tea on the table for each of them to drink when he came back down the stairs. He'd changed into a pair of shorts and a tee-shirt, and she felt distinctly out of place in her wedding gown.

"I should change."

He shook his head. "I like looking at you in that. Unless you're too uncomfortable, of course."

She shrugged. "No, I'm fine. I just figured I should change because you did."

"No need." He took her hand and brought it to his lips. "I'm so glad we're married."

Grace bit her lip nervously. "I'm glad too. I think."

He grinned, stroking the hand his still held with his thumb. "You will be. I'll make sure of it."

They ate slowly, talking about the wedding, and the details she remembered. It had all seemed to happen so quickly that she remembered little of it later. When she finished, she stood to carry her plate to the sink, but he stopped her with a hand on his arm.

"I'll put everything in the sink. You go get ready for bed."

She started to protest that they should watch an episode of the show first, but she was too tired, and she knew it. She couldn't put off her wedding night for another minute. Not if she didn't want to fall asleep in the middle of their lovemaking.

She hurried up the stairs with the box from

Chastity under one arm, disappearing into the master bathroom and taking her hair down from its perfect coiffure. She stripped off the gown, glad there was a zipper that was relatively easy to access running down her back.

Once she'd stripped, she pulled the nightgown over her head and looked at herself in the mirror. It fit perfectly, and the gown matched her eyes to perfection. She wondered idly if Chastity had taken Honor with her to buy the gown so she could match their eyes so well.

When she'd brushed her teeth, she walked into the bedroom to find Marcus sitting at the foot of the bed, waiting for her to come out. She walked over and sat beside him, linking their fingers. "I'm really nervous, but I'm determined not to act like an idiot," she announced softly.

He laughed, bringing her hand to his lips and kissing it. "I'm glad to hear you're not going to act like an idiot. I would rather not have a crying bride on my wedding night." He turned to her, looking into her eyes. "Did you have a chance to talk to Joy?"

She shook her head. "I was too busy this week. Starting a new business is hard work."

"I'm aware," he said with a grin. "Do you want to ask me anything before we start then?" He almost felt like he was teaching her a new game, but he didn't want to scare her in any way. She was too precious to him for that.

"Tell me the rules. Is anything wrong?" She needed clear boundaries. They always made her feel better.

"As far as I'm concerned if we both like it, and it's just between us, nothing is wrong."

She took a deep breath and nodded. "But if you want to do something, and I don't, I can tell you that? I don't have to just let you do it because you're my husband?"

"That's right." He turned to her fully, looking at her in the nightgown. "You look even more beautiful than you did in your wedding dress."

She smiled. "This is what Chastity gave me."

"It matches your eyes perfectly."

"I thought the same thing. She must have taken Honor with her when she shopped for this."

"She's a good sister." He took one finger and trailed it over the spaghetti strap of her gown, down over her chest, and followed the seam to the center of her breast, finding her nipple through the silky fabric.

Grace sucked in a breath at having him touch her so intimately. She put her hands on his shoulders, which were still covered by the fabric of the T-shirt he'd thrown on once they'd gotten home.

Instead of saying anything to her, he pulled away, yanking the shirt over his head and throwing it to the floor. "There. Now you can touch me however you want."

"You don't mind?"

"Mind? I'd beg if you needed me to." He winked at her, leaning down to press his lips to hers while she explored his chest with her fingertips.

She felt strange touching him that way, even

though she knew she was allowed, and he liked it. It still felt slightly wicked to her.

His hands moved down her shoulders and over her arms to her elbows and back up again. She shivered in his arms, loving the feel of his hands on her.

After a moment, he stood up, pulling her to her feet. "We're going to be more comfortable lying down." *And naked*, he wanted to add, but he was afraid of scaring her. It was going to take all the self-control he had to make it through the wedding night.

Leading her to the head of the bed, he pushed one strap of her nightgown off her shoulder and kissed the skin he'd bared, feeling her shudder. "Are you cold?"

"Not one bit. It just feels strange."

"Good strange or bad strange?" he asked.

Her eyes met his. "Good strange. I think."

"You just think? It's my job to make sure you know." He stared down at the nightgown and decided to remove it as if he was ripping off a Band-Aid—quickly. He pushed down the other strap and then with a slight motion had the garment pooling on the floor at her feet

Grace's first instinct was to cover herself, but Marcus caught her hands, looking down at her. "You look so beautiful."

"But—"

"But what?"

"My mother said only a prostitute is ever naked with a man. That a woman of morals only uncovers enough so her man can get to her and do what he needs to do." She wanted to hide from his gaze, but he obviously didn't think there was anything wrong with seeing her this way.

Marcus closed his eyes and counted to ten slowly. "I would like to strangle your mother," he said, his voice calm.

She grinned at that. "I guess you don't agree with her assessment?"

"Not at all. I'm about to get naked too, so if she told you anything about that, get ready to be freaked out."

She put her hand over her mouth to stifle a laugh at his words as he pushed his shorts and underwear down and off. She couldn't believe he'd just announced his intention to take his clothes off. The man surprised her in so many ways.

He sat on the edge of the bed, and pulled her between his legs, his hands cupping her face and bringing it down so he could kiss her. She was so tiny, they were almost on a level, even though he was sitting, and she was standing.

Their kiss quickly turned heated, and his hands roamed over her body, cupping her breasts for just a moment, before flitting away to stroke her shoulders, and then returning to her breasts again a short while later. "Your skin is so soft," he whispered as his lips kissed a trail to her shoulder.

He pulled her onto the bed beside him. "Lie back."

She nodded, doing as he'd asked. She'd been trained to obey her husband, and no matter how nervous she was, she couldn't disobey now.

"I love touching you," he said, pressing kisses from her shoulder down her arm and across to her stomach.

She let out a gasp as his lips settled on her stomach, surprised he was kissing her there. Winding the fingers of one hand through his thick hair, she stroked her other down over his shoulder. "You're making me tingle."

He grinned, looking up at her. "Is that a good thing?"

"Well, I like it, but I'm sure it's wrong." She felt so awkward, wondering what she should do with her hands while he kissed her. Her mother would have said to clench her fists at her sides and send her mind away, but she couldn't do that to Marcus. She knew it would hurt him.

He sighed. "It's supposed to feel good."

"Are you sure?"

"Can you really believe a loving God would give you something that feels good, but tell you that you're not allowed to enjoy it? Does that make any kind of sense to you at all?"

"Well, no, but—"

He moved back up her body to cover her lips with his. "Stop second-guessing yourself." His hands toyed with her body, while he trailed kisses across her face. "You are the most beautiful woman I have ever seen."

She smiled up at him, still feeling conflicted. "Thank you."

His hands grew more insistent as they

traveled down her body, one of them stroking along her hip and over to her core. Her legs were tightly clenched together, so he kissed her again, knowing she would need to be distracted from what he was doing to her. "Relax."

She half-laughed. "I'm lying in a bed naked with a man, who is also naked. Relaxing really isn't an option right now." She wished she could hide from him how very nervous she was.

He put his hand to her side and tickled her, and she immediately started laughing and writhing beside him. He used the opening to move his hand between her legs, stroking her soft folds.

"Hey! That was sneaky!"

"I'm a lawyer. I always find the easiest way to my objective." He brushed his lips against hers again while his hand toyed with her most secret place.

"Why do they bury lawyers under twenty feet of dirt?"

"You've got to be kidding me! Now?"

"Because deep down, they're good people." She grinned at him, stroking his face with her hand.

"If you can think about lawyer jokes, I'm obviously not keeping you busy enough." His mouth descended on hers again, this time more persistently. His hand moved more quickly between her legs, trying to bring her as much pleasure as he could. He knew she wouldn't find much with this first experience, especially with her hang-ups, but it wouldn't stop him from trying.

A few minutes later, he realized she was as

ready as she was going to be. He reached for the foil packet he had on the night stand and dealt with its contents before moving between her legs, cupping her face in his hands, and kissing her.

Grace stared up at him with wide eyes. "I'm scared."

He groaned, burying his face in her neck. "I am too. I'm scared I'm going to disappoint you or hurt you."

His words, for some reason, gave her courage. She put her arms around him and stroked his back. "I'll be all right. I'm tougher than you think."

He grinned at that. If she was being strong for him, she didn't have the time to be worried for herself. He carefully positioned himself, moving inside her with one stroke.

She gasped, wiggling beneath him. "I didn't think you were going to do that yet!"

"And now the scariest part is over."

She nodded, moving under him. "It feels really weird."

"You'll get used to it. I promise." He lowered his lips to hers and started to move inside her.

A short while later, he rolled to his side, still out of breath, holding her tightly to him. "I'm sorry you didn't enjoy it more."

She shook her head. "Women aren't supposed to enjoy it." She felt guilty enough for just doing it. If she'd enjoyed it, she knew it would be much worse.

He closed his eyes with a groan. "You've got to get that out of your head."

"I'm not sure that's possible." She kissed him again, truly glad this first time was over. "I'm going to go shower. I'll be right back."

He propped himself on an elbow and watched her rush from the room. Shower? Was she going to run away to shower every time they made love? The woman seemed to be obsessed with cleanliness.

When she crawled back into his arms a short while later, she was once again wearing the nightgown Chastity had given her. She kissed his lips and settled against him with a smile. She was so glad the dirty part was over, and she could enjoy the rest of the night in her husband's arms.

Chapter Eight

The guilt washed over Grace in waves the moment she woke up the following morning. Marcus was still asleep by her side, and she struggled to control the tears that sprang to her eyes. How did a woman possibly go from believing sex was wrong for her to believing it was right, simply because of a short ceremony?

She rolled so she was facing away from him and let the tears fall. Hopefully by the time he woke up, she'd be done.

An hour later, she had composed herself, and Marcus was still breathing softly in her ear. She crept out of bed and dressed, before going down the stairs to make breakfast for the two of them. None of the other advice her mother had given her seemed to be correct, but maybe her insistence that the way to a man's heart was through his stomach would be. She had to be right about *something!*

Marcus woke to the smell of bacon wafting up from the kitchen, so he quickly dressed and went down the stairs to find his wife in the kitchen putting eggs, bacon and toast on plates for them.

"I didn't know how you like your eggs." Grace found she couldn't meet his eyes after what they'd done the night before. In fact, she wasn't sure she'd ever be able to meet his eyes again. She stared at a point just below his chin instead.

He took the plates from her hand and set them on the counter, kissing her softly. "Good morning."

She smiled, still not meeting his gaze. "Good morning. I hope you're hungry."

He frowned at her, hating that she was having such a hard time with the adjustment from a platonic relationship to marriage. "I am." He carried both of their plates to the table while she poured them coffee and took them to the table.

"Are we going to church this morning?" she asked.

He shook his head. "I don't think so. Not the day after our wedding. We'll go next week." He rarely missed a week in church, but he knew they needed the short time they had together before they returned to work.

She nodded, knowing her parents would never approve, but knowing God would probably understand. "All right."

"Are you excited about meeting Valerie and Jesse later?" he asked, wanting to chase the haunted look from her eyes. She made him feel like he'd done something wrong by making love to his wife.

She grinned, nodding. "But you know, I was thinking about you so much, I'd almost forgotten."

He took her hand and brought it to his lips. "I like hearing that."

"I do care about you a great deal, Marcus. I'm sorry I'm not good at showing it."

"I know you do." He just wished they could

get over the awkwardness. "Have you ever read the Song of Solomon?"

She shook her head. "My parents said that part of the Bible wasn't meant to be read by unmarried girls. We weren't allowed." She'd considered reading it, but there were so many other things she wanted to do with her free time that had nothing to do with reading the Bible.

"Are you kidding me? Where do they get their ideas?"

She sighed. "From the church they raised us in. We weren't allowed to have any real friends either. It was just us and our cousins. No outside influences."

"Wow. Well, you're married now. I want you to read the Song of Solomon. Better, yet, we'll read it together. I want you to see what God's inspired word says about sex. It's all there."

She nodded, biting her lip. "I'm sorry I'm so backward about this. It's just hard to erase a whole life's worth of teaching."

"It is, but we'll work on it together. All right?"

"Yes, of course." She stared intently at her meal as she ate, not wanting to get caught looking at him.

"Can I ask you something?" he asked.

She nodded. "You're my husband. You can ask me anything you want." And she was required to answer with all honesty. She frowned. Being married was harder than she'd realized it would be.

"Are you ever going to look at me again?"

She blushed, raising her gaze to his for the first time all morning. "I'm just embarrassed."

"I know you are, sweetheart, but I don't want you to be. What we did together was a beautiful thing that God created for us to do. You have to get out of your head that it's wrong or dirty, because it's not!"

She shrugged. "Tell my parents that would you?"

"I would love to. What's their phone number?"

Her eyes widened, fear entering them. "Oh no."

"What?"

"I haven't told them I'm married. I need to do that."

He sighed. "We can call them together. Maybe a Skype call?"

"That's how Joy told them she was getting married and introduced them to Kolby."

"Well, then that's what we'll do, but when you're in a better mood. Maybe after we meet with your actor friends this afternoon. Or maybe tomorrow night." *Or maybe never.*

She reached over and gripped his hand. "Have I thanked you yet for not being angry with me for wanting to meet them the day after we marry? I know it's a strange thing."

"It is, but it's also a once in a lifetime opportunity for you. I wouldn't stop you from doing it." He remembered something then. "Are you finished eating?"

She nodded. "Why?"

"I got you a wedding gift, and I want to show it to you." He stood, taking her hand and leading her to the backdoor. Once they were outside, he pointed to a blue-green SUV. "I found you a car to match your eyes."

She laughed. "A car to match my eyes?"

He nodded. "Well, you needed a car, and I know you like to look good. You'll look really good in a car that matches your eyes."

She turned to him, burying her face against his chest. "What did I ever do to deserve a man like you?"

"Well, it must have taken months for you to memorize all those lawyer jokes."

She made a face. "I'm not sure that's a plus, though!"

He shrugged. "Do you want to test drive it?"

"As soon as I do the breakfast dishes."

"Ethel will be really angry if she finds out you did any dishes. She wants you to leave them for her. She thinks you do enough work when you're out of the house."

Grace frowned. "I can't leave the dishes I dirtied for someone else to do tomorrow. That's crazy."

He shrugged. "I think you're going to have to."

"I'll go and rinse them and put them in the sink then. Are you ready to go?"

He nodded. "Yeah, I'm good. I'll probably just wear shorts."

"We'll be home before we go meet Valerie and Jesse, though, right? I want to be wearing a skirt when I meet them."

He caught her by the waist and pulled her to him, kissing her softly. "Sounds good to me."

He grabbed the keys while she put on shoes and got her purse. She'd never driven him, and really had rarely driven at all. Honor had always preferred to be behind the wheel, so she'd happily ridden shotgun everywhere since they'd gotten their licenses.

When they got to the vehicle, she spent a couple of minutes adjusting the seat. "You obviously drove this," she said with a frown. "I feel like a Lilliputian compared to you."

He grinned at her. "Yeah, you do seem awfully tiny. Are you sure you're done growing?"

She glared at him. "If I'm not, what does that say about you?"

"Yeah, let's not go there."

"I was hoping you'd say that." She grinned over at him. "Well, where do you want me to drive?"

He shrugged. "Why don't you just drive toward the mountains, and we'll stop when we feel like it."

She glanced at the clock in the car. It was just past nine. "It feels weird to be out and about on a Sunday morning and not in church."

"Honestly, it does to me too, but we'll do better spending time alone together and getting to know each other better."

She smiled at him before pulling out onto the road. "What do you like to do in your spare time?"

"I don't have a lot of spare time. I work, and then I come home and help out on the ranch when I have time. My foreman and I are trying some new breeding methods, trying to develop heartier, leaner cattle."

"That sounds…fun!"

He laughed softly. "Almost as much fun as watching *Lazy Love*?"

"Well, you know I'm biased about that show."

"Only a little." While they drove, he explained about the different things they saw, telling little stories about places he'd been along the way. "We went on a field trip where we had a picnic at that river once," he said pointing off to the right.

"It looks beautiful. I'd picnic there."

"Maybe we can do that on Saturday."

She frowned. "Didn't I tell you? We set our schedule so we'll always be closed on Mondays, but open on Saturdays."

"That stinks for me. Maybe I can make Saturday a day for paperwork and try not to schedule clients on Mondays going forward."

"I'd really like that if you can make it happen. If not, I completely understand."

After they'd reached the base of the mountains, he had her turn around on a side road. "I don't want you to try to navigate the mountains until you're used to this vehicle."

She frowned at that. "I'm not sure I'll ever

feel up to driving in the mountains."

"We'll have to see. It's kind of important to be able to do that around here."

"I can see why." She concentrated on the road as she pulled back out to head toward the ranch. "When will I get to meet your parents?"

He frowned. "I guess I should tell them I'm married, huh? Although I'm sure Grandma already has."

"Will they be mad we didn't wait so they could be there?"

"Nah. They eloped. They don't think anyone should have to go through the stress of a big wedding." He stared out the window. "I got engaged in college, and we were going through the stress of wedding planning, and Mom kept telling me to just run off with her and marry her, but she wouldn't go for it."

"What happened?" She really couldn't imagine him being engaged to someone, and even though it was years before, she felt a bit jealous at the idea.

"Car wreck. She was hit by a drunk driver and killed."

"I'm so sorry. What was her name?" She felt terrible for her momentary jealousy. It had been a long time before, but no one deserved to die that way.

"Erin. Erin Krol." He hated to think of her and how she'd looked the last time he'd seen her, all broken in a hospital bed.

"Tell me about her."

He shrugged. "She was a nursing student. One of the most sarcastic people I've ever met in my life. Fun to be around. She was always on some kind of crusade to help others."

"Do you still miss her?"

"She died six years ago. I loved her with everything inside me, but memories fade. I think she would have been a good wife for me, but I'm not unhappy that I'm moving on with my life without her."

Grace nodded. "You'll have to show me her picture when we get home."

"I can do that." Marcus felt strange talking to her about Erin. She seemed to have been a lifetime ago to him. "Does it bother you I never mentioned her?"

"Well, considering we've only known each other for a week, I'm sure there are a lot of things we'll learn as we go. It's the nature of marrying so quickly."

"Do you regret marrying so fast?"

She shook her head. "Absolutely not. I'm still a little shy around you." At his laugh, she sighed. "Okay, so I'm still *a lot* shy around you, but I'll get over that in time."

"I'm sure you will. I'll help."

"How will you help?"

He grinned, glad she was paying attention to the road. "Oh, I have some ideas…"

"Forget it. I don't trust your ideas." Grace pulled into his driveway and parked the car, breathing a sigh of relief she was finished driving.

"I'm glad I won't have to drive much further than the Culpepper Ranch on a regular basis. I really don't like driving."

"I guess I can drop you off at the bakery every day if you really need me to."

"Absolutely not. I can do it. I'm just not fond of it. I want to be able to drive when I need to."

She opened the door and slid out of the car, heading toward the house. "Are you hungry? Should I fix lunch?"

He shrugged. "I could eat. It's noon, so if we want to eat before we go, we should do it now. We'll need to leave at about one-thirty to get there when you want to."

"I'm really excited and really nervous to meet them both."

"Have you ever met a celebrity?"

She shook her head. "Well, I met this woman who travels around teaching women's Bible studies once, and my mother totally fangirled her, but I've never met anyone famous whom I cared to meet."

"Am I allowed to ask for pictures of them with you?"

"I'll hate you forever if you don't," she said with a wink, wandering into the kitchen and finding something to fix. "Would sandwiches be all right? Then I'll have time to shower and change before we leave."

"Sure. I don't care." He eyed her for a moment. "Exactly how many times per day do you shower?" She seemed to always be showering to him.

"Oh, you know how I was raised. Cleanliness is next to godliness and all that."

"That's not really answering my question."

"At least twice a day. Sometimes more."

He raised an eyebrow at that. "Are you OCD or something?"

"Not at all. I just like to be clean and neat. I get messy with all the flour that I'm constantly working with, so I shower before and after work. Then it kind of seems to carry over onto the weekends too. There's nothing wrong with that, is there?"

"No, of course not." He sat on the counter and watched as she put sandwiches together. "Thanks for fixing lunch."

"It's not really called fixing lunch when it's only sandwiches," she said, rolling her eyes.

"It is when you cut them into nice little triangles and serve them on real plates."

"What would you have done? Fake plates?"

"I'd probably have eaten it from a paper towel while standing up in the kitchen."

She laughed. "Well, I guess we can stand in the kitchen to eat them if that makes you happy. I was planning on going into the dining room, though."

He grinned. "I'm just not going to bother with the table when it's only me."

"But since there are two of use, the table is acceptable?" she asked, a grin on her face.

"Well, sure!"

They carried their plates to the table and she

went back to the kitchen to get some tea for each of them. When she returned, she found him watching her. "What?"

He shrugged. "Just thinking about how beautiful you are."

She blushed at that. She hoped he wasn't remembering what she'd looked like while they were—she felt her face flame even brighter.

"What are you thinking?"

She shrugged, avoiding his gaze again.

"Tell me."

"It's nothing."

"It's obviously not nothing, or you'd tell me. What's going on in that head of yours?"

"I was hoping you weren't thinking about what I looked like while we were—you know."

He grinned. "No, I don't know. While we were what?"

She glared at him. "I'm not going to say it, and you can't make me."

"While we were making love? It's not dirty or wicked, you know."

She shrugged. "I wish I could convince myself of that. It's not as easy as you make it sound."

"We'll work on it."

She finished eating and picked up their plates, rinsing them and putting them in the sink. "I'll be back in a few. I need to get ready."

"Is it okay if I wear this?"

She shrugged. "You can wear whatever you want."

He looked down at himself with a frown as she left the room. He knew enough about women to know that what she really meant was she wanted him to change. Fine. If it would make her happy, he could put on a pair of slacks and a nice shirt. It wouldn't kill him.

Chapter Nine

Grace dressed carefully in a skirt and blouse, fixing her hair and make-up before leaving the bathroom. She found Marcus sitting on the bed, reading a book, obviously waiting on her. "Do I look all right?" she asked worriedly.

His eyes drifted from her perfectly fixed hair, down to her toes and back. "You look so beautiful I don't want anyone else to see you. I think I'll keep you here and have my way with you." He rolled off the bed and got to his feet, walking toward her. His hands went to her waist and he pulled her toward him.

"Don't smudge my lipstick!" she protested as his head was descending toward hers.

"Really? I can't kiss you? We haven't even been married for twenty-four hours yet!"

She sighed. "Fine. Kiss me, and then I'll fix my lipstick. I think we have enough time."

"I don't want to kiss you now." He made a face at her. "Can't believe you won't let me kiss you just because you put makeup on. I'll have you know I'm an excellent lipstick blotter."

She pulled his head down to hers, kissing him. "Sorry. I'll remember next time to just wait to put my lipstick on until after we've kissed." She hurried back into the bathroom to fix her lipstick and brought out a washcloth, washing her lipstick off him. "There. Now you look all manly again."

"I don't look manly with your lipstick on?"

She shook her head. "No, not very." She looked him up and down, approving of his clothes. "You look much better now."

He slipped his arm around her waist, steering her toward the door. "Let's go meet your people."

"My heart is beating so fast, it feels like it's going to jump out of my chest."

"How come you didn't feel that way last night?"

She blushed. "I did. I just didn't tell you I felt that way."

"Tell me next time, would you? It's good for my ego."

"I don't think your ego needs any help at all."

Marcus frowned. "Are you saying I have a swelled head?"

She shrugged. "If the hat doesn't fit…"

He sighed. "I get no respect. I expected to be treated this way after ten years of marriage, but not the first day!"

"Do you know how to save a drowning lawyer?"

"Please God, save me from lawyer jokes!"

"Take your foot off his head."

He groaned, but refused to respond to her. Maybe if he quit reacting, she'd quit telling the awful jokes.

They got into his truck and he drove them the

twenty minutes into town. "I really am nervous," she said as they saw the buildings that indicated they were almost to the diner. "What if they hate me?"

"Well, they already practically know you from all you say to them on Twitter, right?"

"Almost." She'd wanted to meet up with other LLers before, because they sometimes met to watch the current episodes, but her parents had never allowed it, so she'd never met anyone from online. "You know they say you can never really know someone just from meeting them online."

He shrugged. "I don't know if that's true. I think you can get to know someone really well without the trappings of real life being in the way. Of course, some people do misrepresent themselves online."

"I know." She took a deep breath. "I don't know what they'd get out of it though. I'm still not sure why they're in town, but I'm so excited to get to actually meet them."

Marcus parked the car and led her into the diner. She had never been there, and she looked around. "Do we seat ourselves?"

He nodded. "Why don't we grab that booth in the corner?"

She followed him to it, waiting until he slid in and then she sat beside him. "I always think couples look stupid when they sit on the same side of a booth with no one across from them. Like they're so intent on looking like they're in love they can't get out of each other's pockets for even a minute."

He grinned at her assessment. "I think you

may be right. There's a reason this time, though, so even if we look stupid, we'll have to live through it."

Grace had taken the side of the booth where she could see people come and go from the diner. When the door opened, and the bell over it tinkled, she saw Valerie and Jesse Savoy walk in. "That's them," she hissed at Marcus.

"Well, get up and introduce yourself then. You'll have an easier time recognizing them than they will recognizing you."

Grace took a deep breath and stood, walking over to the couple. "Hi, I'm Grace." She wanted to hug the other woman, but she had no idea how Valerie would feel about it.

Valerie's face transformed into a grin, and she reached out to hug Grace. "It's so nice to meet you."

Grace smiled shyly. "It's good to meet you too. Come over and meet my husband."

"You said you got married yesterday? That's wonderful." Valerie followed her over, and she waited as Jesse slid into the booth.

Grace found herself mesmerized by the couple she'd seen so often onscreen. "You guys have just as much chemistry in real life."

Valerie laughed. "We do." She looked at Marcus. "Do you watch our show as well?"

He nodded. "Grace has just introduced me to it. We've watched the first half of the first season now. I just saw the episode where you kiss for the first time. You two are something else."

Jesse grinned. "I'll never forget filming that."

He got a faraway look on his face, and Valerie elbowed him.

"Stop. They don't need to hear about that." Valerie focused her attention on Grace. "I had to come after I saw your picture of the sunset and the mountains. We got in yesterday. This is such a beautiful place."

"How long are you here for?"

Valerie sighed. "We fly out tonight at ten. We'll have to sleep the whole way back to Texas, so we can film in the morning." She rubbed the back of her neck, looking tired.

"How are you feeling?"

Valerie grinned, her hand reaching out to take Jesse's. "I'm good. Morning sickness is giving me fits, and sometimes I feel like the only thing keeping me put together are the clothes on my back. Baby's growing and getting healthy, though, so I can't complain. Well, I *could*, but I won't."

Grace smiled at that. "I'm glad you decided to meet me while you were here. I was so excited to get your tweet. I wasn't sure if I should, but Marcus was all for it."

"Why weren't you sure?"

"Well, we only have one full day off together before we go back to work. So we married last night, and today is it."

"Oh! I knew you married yesterday, but I guess I just assumed you'd take a week off or something." Valerie frowned.

"Like you did, right?" Grace asked, knowing the story of the other couple's marriage on a Friday night and going back to work on Monday morning.

"Oh, yeah, just like us." Valerie laughed. "We're looking for a new house. We don't want to raise a child in California. We like the area of Texas we're in, but we don't want to be there all the time. So when we saw your sunset picture, we came to see the town you mentioned."

"Really? Did you find a place you like?"

Valerie nodded, her eyes bright. "We found this little ranch we want to buy. We don't really want it to be a ranch, but we'll find a buyer for the cattle. They seem to come with it. The amount of land is just perfect for us to have the privacy we need, but also good for raising a child."

"Whose ranch are you buying?" Marcus asked. He'd been careful to keep quiet, so Grace could enjoy them, but he had to speak up then.

"Some guy named Jones? I don't know," Jesse answered. "You know him?"

"I do! I've been eyeing his herd." Marcus thought for a moment. "I'm a lawyer, but I've taken over my dad's ranch. I'm not really part of the day to day operations, but I'm involved in the big decisions. If you don't want those cattle, we can work something out."

Jesse smiled over at Valerie. "Seems like someone wants us to move here."

"Other than me, you mean?" Grace asked.

Valerie smiled at her. "Jesse wasn't all for us meeting like this, but I told him we'd been following each other on Twitter for years. He finally seemed to understand then."

Jesse shrugged, looking at Marcus. "I don't know that I'll ever really trust anyone with my wife, but since she said I could come…"

Marcus nodded emphatically. "I feel like it's my job to take care of Grace."

Grace rolled her eyes at Valerie. "Now I want to ditch them and go get our own table. Being petite and female does not equal being weak."

Valerie laughed. "That's always been my favorite thing about you on Twitter. I love your sense of humor."

"Thanks." Grace reached down for a small basket she'd brought with her. "You're going to like me better for this." She set the basket on the table between them.

A waitress stopped at the table then, before Valerie could lift the cloth napkin covering the basket to look. "What'll ya have?"

"Just coffee for me," Grace said.

Marcus smiled. "Hi, Tabitha. How're the kids?"

The waitress smiled at Marcus. "Exhausting! Is this the new wife I heard about?"

Marcus nodded. "Grace, this is Tabitha. She and Karlan were in the same grade in school. Tabitha, my wife, Grace." He had to stifle the prideful grin that toyed at his lips when he introduced her as his wife.

"So nice to meet you." Tabitha looked back at Marcus, a smile on her face now. "What do you want?"

"Get me a Coke and the fried cheese sticks. I

feel like coating my arteries good today."

Tabitha turned to Valerie next. For a moment, she had a blank stare, and then her eyes widened. "You're Valerie Dobson!" Her eyes flicked back and forth between Jesse and Valerie.

Valerie smiled. "It's Valerie Savoy now, but yes." Valerie reached down to grab her purse, pulling something from it. "I'd like a glass of water and a salad."

"Yes, ma'am. No problem, ma'am." Tabitha's eyes went to Jesse. "And you?"

Jesse pointed at Marcus. "I'll have what he's having."

As soon as she'd gone, Valerie quickly signed the picture she had taken from her purse before handing it to Jesse. After he'd scrawled his name, she put it on the edge of the table.

Then she lifted the napkin from the basket to see the fresh muffins and cinnamon rolls. "Oh, those look delicious."

"I opened a bakery with two of my cousins this week. We make those, so when you move to town, you need to make sure to come by often."

"We will." Valerie handed Jesse the basket, and he set it on a ledge beside the booth. "We brought you something too."

Grace smiled. "Really?"

Valerie nodded. "I have a full cast poster for you, and I had everyone sign it."

"Oh, wow! Thank you!" Grace was more than a little impressed the actress had thought to bring her something. "That's the perfect gift for me!"

"It's in the car, but I'll give it to you when we go."

"I'm excited!"

Marcus looked at Jesse. "I guess I'm going to sleep with you looking down at me now."

Jesse laughed. "Fans are fickle creatures. It'll be gone in a month."

Grace frowned at Jesse. "It will not! I've followed the show since the second season."

"Not the first?" Jesse asked, a bit surprised by that.

Grace shook her head. "We didn't have a television at home, so I found it through Netflix. I always buy the current season on Amazon, but I have to watch it the next morning."

"Now you can watch it as it comes on," Marcus reminded her.

"Just another reason I'm glad we're married," Grace said with a grin.

Tabitha came back to the table with drinks and thanked Valerie over and over for the autographs. "My husband's never going to believe I actually met you two."

"You have proof now," Valerie said, nodding at her hands.

After Tabitha hurried away, Jesse looked at Grace. "We'll move here on our next week off, which is in two weeks. We'll have to have dinner then."

Valerie smiled at Grace. "That means he approves of me talking to you, and we can hang out."

"I'd love that! Why don't y'all plan to come to our house for dinner when you come back? I'd love to cook for you." Grace made the offer and then hoped she could talk Ethel into giving up her kitchen for one night.

"Just so you're a better cook than Jo." Valerie winked at Grace. Her character, Jo, was known for trying to cook and filling the entire house with smoke.

Grace laughed, rolling her eyes. "Anyone is a better cook than Jo."

*****

After dinner that night, Grace curled into Marcus's side on the couch. "Thank you so much for being so kind about today. You didn't have to let me meet them."

"It was worth it to me to see you so happy." He stroked his hand up and down her arm.

She smiled. "You're a good husband."

"I try to be." He turned to kiss her, his tongue stroking out to touch hers.

When she wrapped her arms around his neck and responded, he pulled her onto his lap, astride him. She pulled away, blushing. "We can't kiss like this down here."

He frowned. "Why not?"

"Because we can only do that in bed." How could he not realize that?

"Grace, we're married. We can make love in the living room of our own home if we want to. I wouldn't want to if Ethel were here, but she won't be in until morning, so we can do it here now if we want to." He pulled her back down for a kiss.

She pulled away from him in shock. "But the lights are on."

He shook his head. "It's okay for me to see you naked, you know."

She blushed. "You did last night, and my mother would have a fit if she knew."

"I guess I didn't make it clear last night, but your parents are not allowed to be part of our love life. You have my permission to forget they exist every time I start kissing you."

"I'm not sure that's possible." She frowned, closing her eyes. "I feel so guilty every time we touch. Kissing doesn't seem to bother me, but when you touch me in other places, or when I sit on you like this, I just feel terribly wicked."

He sighed. "Well, we're going to be wicked, I'm afraid." He brought her lips back to his, kissing her passionately. "If you are that worried about doing this out of bed, let's go upstairs."

She nodded, getting off his lap and climbing the stairs to their bedroom.

He closed the door, and for her benefit shut off the light, before he stripped off his clothes and made short work of hers.

He lowered her onto the bed, taking a condom from the nightstand and laying it beside them, so he wouldn't have to reach too far for it later. His hands and lips were all over her, stroking her to a fever pitch.

This time he pulled her astride him, sitting

with his back to the headboard, stroking her continuously as he taught her how to move in a way that would bring them both pleasure.

He had a trickle of sweat running down his cheek when he felt her clench around him. He groaned, moving swiftly to finish himself, clutching her to him.

He rained kisses on her face, thrilled that she'd finished that time. He hadn't been sure he'd be able to make that happen with her hang-ups.

Grace lay against him, eyes closed, wanting to scream at the emotional pain. She wasn't supposed to enjoy sex. It was wrong.

After a minute, she kissed his cheek. "I'm going to go shower." *And throw up.*

He sighed as he watched her go, hating that she thought such a beautiful experience required an immediate shower afterward. He sat there for a moment, hating himself for making love with his beautiful bride.

He heard the shower start, and then he heard loud sobs coming from the bathroom. He debated for a moment whether he should go to her or just pretend he didn't know. In the end, he knew he had to help her if there was any way he could.

He went into the bathroom and climbed into the shower with her, pulling her into his arms. He didn't mention her tears, and he didn't allow her to pull away. He just held her while she sobbed hysterically.

Finally, when the water started to turn cold, he shut off the stream and stepped out of the tub, wrapping her in the towel she'd set out. He carefully dried her off as if she was a child, brushing out her long hair and blow-drying it for her.

When they got back into bed, he stroked her back, feeling her exhaustion. When she slept, she made little hiccupping sounds, as if she was still fighting the tears.

Marcus hated that he'd made her feel that way. He loved her so much. There was a big decision he needed to make, and he needed to make it soon. He'd either have to stop making love with her or find some way for her to get beyond the emotions that her upbringing was causing her.

He couldn't let her keep beating herself up over it. There had to be a solution.

*****

While Grace was at the doctor the following day, he went home and talked to Ethel. "I need you to do something for me."

Ethel seemed to ignore him for a moment as she continued to clean the kitchen. "You already unhappy with your new bride?"

He shook his head. "No, I love her." He sighed. "Her parents managed to convince her that lovemaking is wicked. She thinks if she enjoys it at all she's going to hell or something ridiculous like that. Can you talk to her?"

Ethel raised an eyebrow at him. "What makes you think I'm the one to talk to her?"

He frowned. "You had eight children, and you were a pastor's wife. Surely you've had sex once or twice." He hated talking to his grandmother's friend about this, but it was easier than talking to his grandmother herself. He'd do that next if it became necessary.

"At least twice. And you know what?" she asked, her voice a whisper.

He didn't want to know what. He really didn't. He knew he was about to find out though. "What?"

"I liked it. A lot."

"I don't want to know that!"

Ethel cackled loudly. "Yeah, I'll talk to your little princess. When I'm done with her, she'll think it's wrong not to enjoy it."

Marcus shook his head. "Just help her, please."

"No problem!"

Chapter Ten

When Grace got home from the doctor, she wandered into the kitchen to grab a snack. She hadn't spent much time exploring the contents of the kitchen yet. She had seen a car parked outside that she thought probably belonged to Ethel. It had been there when she'd met her previously.

As she dug through the refrigerator, she heard a sniff. "Don't move things around in there. You live here now, but the kitchen is still my territory."

Grace straightened up and smiled at Ethel. "I understand, and I'll do my best. I cooked a couple of meals over the weekend, and I even left the dishes for you."

Ethel grinned. "Was that hard for you?"

"It was awful. I felt like I was betraying my mother and God, and I was going to go straight to hell!" Grace was exaggerating, but only a little. Every little sin was hell-worthy to her parents.

"Sounds like you had an interesting upbringing. I can only imagine what they told you about married life." Ethel shook her head. "I was a minister's wife for fifty years. I have counseled women who came from very strict households. Do you realize some even thought that enjoying sex with their husbands is wrong?"

Grace blinked a couple of times. "They do?"

"Not anymore they don't. I set them real straight on that." Ethel got herself a glass of water and leaned against the counter. "I had eight kids, and trust me, I enjoyed conceiving every single one of them."

Grace smiled, feeling uncomfortable, but knowing this woman might be able to help her. "And you didn't feel like it was wrong?" If a pastor's wife didn't think it was wrong, maybe it wasn't. She hoped she could get past this somehow.

"Why would something that God created, that feels so dang good, be wrong? Really, some of those women had mothers who told them to lie back and plan their grocery lists. Just makes me sick to my stomach to think some women try to brainwash their daughters that way."

Grace bit her lip, not wanting to admit how she felt, but deciding this woman would be safe. She had to talk to someone about it. "Can you keep something confidential?"

"Oh, honey. You never need to ask that of a minister's wife. We learn to keep stuff to ourselves fast."

"My mom taught me that sex is dirty and enjoying sex, even with your husband, is wicked." Grace looked down at her hands, embarrassed to have the conversation, but she hated disappointing Marcus so much. "I threw up last night, because I felt so guilty for liking it."

Ethel shook her head. "Your mother needs to be put before a firing squad. There's nothing wrong with liking sex, honey. Not one little thing. In fact, God must have intended for us to like sex, 'cuz it feels so darn good. Have you ever read the Song of Solomon?"

"No, ma'am. Mama said that single women were forbidden to read that book."

"Of course she did. Trust me, you should read it. It's filled with very interesting information about sexual relations. If you believe the Bible is inspired by God, and I'm sure you do, then you'll see that He intended for us to enjoy it by reading that book." Ethel took Grace's hand. "Trust me, honey. You're not the first person to have been raised by someone preaching that nonsense, and you won't be the last. Do yourself and your new husband a favor and fight the guilt. I think it's more wrong to withhold from your husband the pleasure you feel."

"Really? You do?"

"Definitely. Do you think Marcus can enjoy making love with you when he knows how upset it makes you? If he knows you're throwing up from the guilt? That's not fair to him or to you."

Grace sighed, feeling a tear prick her eye. "It's just so strange to me. I was taught that birth control is wrong as well, but Marcus says it's fine."

"Marcus is right! You've been married for two days. If you want children right away, then you should have them. If you want time alone with your husband before the children come, then you should use birth control."

"But—are you sure? My parents say that having sex without the thought of having children is against God."

"Let's take just a minute to face facts, Grace. Your parents are morons. Plain and simple." Ethel shook her head in disgust. "I don't criticize the way people parent often, but your parents? They're idiots. Please tell me there are no more girls at home."

Grace shook her head. "Actually all six of us are here in Culpepper now. Four married the Culpepper brothers, I've married Marcus, and my sister is going to marry Angus tomorrow."

Ethel nodded approvingly. "All good men. You'll all be so much better off without your parents' influence."

Grace frowned. "Will I ever get over the idea that what I'm doing is wrong?"

"If you let yourself, you will. You need to think of making love as a way to express your love to your husband. A God-given way of expressing it, and one that He made to be wonderful."

"I'll try."

"Did you bring your Bible with you?"

Grace nodded. "Of course. I always have my Bible."

"I challenge you to read Song of Solomon before Marcus comes home tonight. I promise you, you'll look at things differently when you're done."

"I will then. If you really think it'll help."

Ethel took the steps between them, hugging Grace. "I know you want to please him. You're a good girl, Grace."

After she'd gone, Grace found a snack, before

lifting the lid of the crock-pot and sniffing the food cooking there. Then she went into the living room and grabbed the Bible from the bookshelf. It wasn't hers, but that didn't really matter to her. As long as she had one.

She flipped through the Bible to the Song of Solomon and began reading, determined to get through the whole book before Marcus got home from work. Glancing at the clock, she saw it was only three, so she should be able to do it if it wasn't too long.

As she read, she was both surprised at the contents and shocked that her mother had deemed it inappropriate reading for her. When she finished, she closed the Bible and set it aside, spending a few moments staring off into space and thinking about what she'd read.

After thinking for a while, she reached for her phone and dialed her parents in Kentucky. Her mother answered. "Hi, Mom. It's Grace."

"Gracie! It's so good to hear your voice. How are your sisters doing?"

"We're all fine." Grace paused for a moment, working out how to formulate her question. "Mom, what scriptures have you read to prove that women shouldn't enjoy sex?"

"Grace Quinlan! That is not a topic for an unmarried young lady!"

"I'm Grace Wells now, Mom. I got married on Saturday. What scriptures?"

Her mother sputtered for a moment. "You got married? Who is this man? Is he a Christian?"

"Yes. His grandfather is a pastor. What scriptures?"

Her mother was silent. "I have seen no actual scriptures, but that's what the pastor says, and we know he's right about these things."

Grace closed her eyes, wanting to scream. "So when you told us that enjoying sex within marriage was against God, you were lying to us?"

"It wasn't a lie! No Christian woman would ever enjoy sex!"

Grace took a deep breath. She wanted to reach through the phone and choke her mother. "I'm not sure I have anything else to say to you, Mom. Good night."

"Grace, don't you dare hang up this phone! I need to know about the man you married!"

Grace ended the call and put her phone down. Her entire life she'd believed her family just followed the scriptures more strictly than others did. To find out she'd been lied to made her furious.

She looked at the clock on the wall. Marcus would be home at any moment. She needed to calm down before he walked in the door, so she went upstairs to shower, ignoring the phone that kept ringing and ringing. Yes, she knew she showered more than was normal, but for her, water was calming. And right then, that's what she needed more than anything.

When she got out of the shower, she put on a pair of shorts and a T-shirt, her mind still grappling with both the phone call with her mother and the Song of Solomon.

She went downstairs to find Marcus just coming in the front door. "Hi."

Marcus smiled at her, walking to her and kissing her softly. He set something down, but she ignored it. A husband was allowed to have secrets after all. "Hi. How was your day?"

"Interesting." She walked into the kitchen and dished the casserole Ethel had made out onto two plates.

"What did the doctor have to say?" he asked.

She shrugged. "I'm healthy. We decided on the shot for birth control, so I don't have to worry about trying to remember to take a pill every day. She said we needed to use other precautions for at least a week."

"We can do that." He sat down at the table and smiled as she sat beside him. "I brought you a present."

She looked at him with a grin. "I hope it's not something else as expensive as a car."

He shook his head. "Nope, not a car. I'll give it to you after dinner."

She leaned toward him and kissed him softly. "You spoil me."

"I think everyone needs to be spoiled at some point in their lives. It's your turn."

After the meal, she rinsed the dishes and put them in the sink before joining him on the couch. He handed her a wrapped box, and she turned it over in her hands, shaking it slightly as she tried to guess what it could possibly be.

"Stop! Just open it!" Marcus was laughing as

he shook his head at her.

Grace smiled. "I like the anticipation when I open a gift."

"Obviously. I want to see my wife's face when she opens it. Hurry up!"

She giggled, sliding a finger under the paper and carefully tearing it. She didn't really care about saving the paper, but she knew it was driving him crazy, which was fun!

Finally, she had the present in her hands, and she stared down into a framed picture of her with Valerie and Jesse Savoy. The couple was on either side of her, and they each had an arm around her. "Oh, it's wonderful!"

"That's why I was a little late getting home. I had that done today."

"I've never received anything that I will treasure quite so much."

He grinned, thinking about the huge cardboard cutout of the picture he'd ordered that would be delivered in a week or two. "I'm glad you like it."

"Like it? I love it!" She carefully set the photo on the coffee table before flinging herself into his arms.

Marcus closed his arms around his wife, loving her enthusiastic thanks. His hands stroked her back. "I missed you while I was working today."

She grinned. "I missed you too." And she had. She was surprised by just how much she loved him after such a short time knowing him. She just hoped he could forgive her for how silly she'd acted. She got to her feet and grabbed his hand. "Let's go upstairs."

He raised an eyebrow at that, but he was sure she couldn't mean what he wanted her to mean by her words. She led him up the stairs, holding his hand tightly in hers. When they reached the bedroom, Grace closed the door, before turning to him.

Without a word, she pulled her T-shirt over her head before unfastening her shorts. After she'd divested herself of her bra and panties, she went to work on his clothes, doing her best to ignore the shocked look on his face.

Marcus couldn't believe this was the same woman he'd married. What was going on in her head? He was afraid to ask and break the spell.

Thirty minutes later, he lay in the bed, holding her close in his arms. "Do you want to talk about what that was about?"

She looked up at him, love shining from her eyes. "It was about two things, actually."

"Okay. Two things. And they are?"

"The first was apologizing for being a ninny the past couple of days. I talked to Ethel today, and I read the Song of Solomon, and then I called my mother."

"Wait, you called your mother? Why did you call your mother?"

"Because I wanted her to tell me which scriptures told her that it was wrong for a woman to enjoy making love with her husband." She held his eyes as she talked about it, surprising him even more than her sudden attack on his person.

"What did she tell you?" He was honestly curious to know. He'd never understood why some people felt that enjoying sex was so wrong.

"That she'd never seen actual scriptural backing for the belief, but because the pastor talked about it, she knew it has to be true." She shook her head. "All this time, it's been a lie, and I believed it!"

He nodded, smiling slightly. She didn't seem the least bit upset about making love with him tonight. She hadn't even run for the shower yet, which was a very good sign. "What's the second reason?"

She grinned, and he could see the hint of a siren in her eyes. "The second reason was pleasure, plain and simple."

He gathered her close, burying his face in her neck. "I'm so glad you sorted this out for yourself."

She nodded. "So am I! I thought I'd spend the rest of my life vomiting every time we made love, and I don't think that was acceptable to either one of us."

He closed his eyes. "Did you vomit last night?" He hated that he'd caused that much mental anguish for her.

"Yeah. But I didn't tonight." She stroked his face. "Thank you so much for putting up with my silly insecurities. I've never in my life felt so much for anyone."

"Felt so much for anyone? What exactly does that mean? I'm a lawyer, so you'd better speak slowly."

She giggled. "It means I love you. I love you so much. I think I knew you were the man for me from the instant you kissed me. I'm so glad you put up with all my nonsense to get us to this point."

He sighed happily. Kissing her again, he stroked her cheek with his hand. "I love you too, Grace. I knew the moment I laid eyes on you." He winked at her. "I'm not sure I could have put up with the lawyer jokes for so long otherwise."

"Lawyer jokes? What lawyer jokes?"

He laughed, sitting up in bed and pulling her up with him. "We should probably watch a little more *Lazy Love* before we go to sleep, shouldn't we? I mean, now that I've met the main stars, I'm a bit more invested in the show."

"I knew it! I knew you'd love it as much as I did, and you just had to give it a chance!"

He shrugged. "It's growing on me a bit." Anything that made her that happy, he would watch whether he liked it or not. But the truth was, *Lazy Love* wasn't nearly as bad as he thought it would be. And doing it with her made everything just right.

Made in the USA
Coppell, TX
18 October 2025

61401707R00085